Spells and Shadows

A Pride and Prejudice Fantasy Variation

Victoria Kincaid

Chapter One

Darcy crept through the underbrush, placing each foot carefully, all too aware that any misstep could cause a snapped twig or other noise. He gathered shadows around his body, rendering him nearly impossible to glimpse—even with the full moon. But his magic could do nothing to muffle sounds.

Fortunately, the gathering in the clearing was generating enough noise of its own; the sounds of chanting filtered through the trees. *Apparently Benjamin Tolliver's information had been accurate*, Darcy thought. *Good. It had cost enough.*

Towering pine trees edged the clearing, which was illuminated by a roaring bonfire as well as moonlight. The robed figures had assembled a crude circle of stones, none bigger than a human head. Darcy was shocked to find approximately twenty men; he had expected perhaps a dozen. And no doubt some were not present today.

His cousin, Richard Fitzwilliam, who had recruited Darcy into the Assessor's Agency, had only recently learned of this group's existence and sent Darcy to investigate. Richard expected a small group; he would not be pleased to hear about these numbers. Darcy had hoped to disrupt their activity, but he could not do much alone against so many mages.

Well, Darcy would gather as much information as he could about the illicit magical activity and relay it to Richard, who would relay it to Viscount Cranston, the director of the Agency. Cranston would decide what to do about the group.

Darcy crept to the edge of the clearing, concealing himself behind a tall bush. He needed to identify the participants. Everyone wore gray robes with hoods shadowing their faces, but Darcy had been born with the power to manipulate shadows. He pushed and peeled them away—slowly and gently so that nobody would notice—to reveal the participants' identities.

The Earl of Cassing's second son, the younger brother of Viscount Fletchley, the third son of Dalloway, a well-known sugar magnate, and Tolliver himself—the second son of an admiral. Others were unfamiliar to Darcy, but he was certain they were the same ilk: disgruntled young men with too much time on their hands and insufficient funds.

Unfortunately, the leader, who stood on a wooden platform a little removed from the others, and a dozen of the participants wore masks that appeared to be Egyptian in origin—although Darcy doubted they were anything close to authentic. He had no way of identifying those men or knowing if they were people he would recognize.

The words of the chant that he could discern sounded like Latin. The leader would call out a phrase, and the others would echo it. *At least these young men are wringing some use from their expensive classical educations.*

Darcy noticed no clues about the leader's identity. Tolliver had not known the man's name, which was apparently a closely guarded secret. Twice he had almost backed out of meeting Darcy, who had been forced to double the amount he paid the informant. Even so, Tolliver had been pale and nervous when he met Darcy in the town of Luton.

The chanting reached a fever pitch, causing the very air of the clearing to pulse with magical power as the flames rose higher than the men's heads. This unfamiliar magic prickled at the back of Darcy's neck; he drew more shadows around himself. This group would not be forgiving if they discovered him now.

The leader's voice rose as the chanting died down. He must have purchased a far-speaking charm, allowing him to project his voice but distorting it at the same time. The words were intelligible but somewhat sonorous and slow. "My friends! The Council and their enforcers at the Agency have long told us that each mancer must limit himself to one kind of magic." Darcy leaned forward. That was what the Council for Enchantment taught because that was how magic worked. Each mage was born with one mancy.

The leader continued. "But, they lie! Through assiduous study, I have developed new magical powers! Powers that the mancers on the Council can only dream of!"

The listeners were silent, utterly entranced as they absorbed the leader's words. Darcy could practically feel their excitement at the idea that they could develop additional magics. Even he found the idea appealing, although he doubted the leader could follow through on what he promised. If he indeed had developed new powers, it was using methods that were illegal—methods that always relied on pain, blood, and death.

"But we will not be bound by their shackles!" the leader cried. "We long to reach our fullest potential! Today they force us to exercise our magic in secret. But soon we will do so where everyone will know!"

The men cheered, but Darcy shuddered. What did the leader mean by that? Practicing dark mancy openly? How was that possible? The only situations Darcy could imagine would give him nightmares for weeks.

"Today you will witness a demonstration of a mere fraction of the power I have developed. I have summoned a new kind of servant to our cause!" The leader lifted his hand which held an amulet dangling from a gold chain. Darcy's informant had told him the amulet was carved with the image of Anubis, the Egyptian god of the underworld. The medallion twisted in the wind, catching the light in flickers. "Observe what I can do now that I have unleashed my full power!"

The leader laid the amulet on a tall rock at the outer edge of the circle. Then, taking up an earthenware jar, he poured a dark liquid over it. Blood. Darcy could only hope it was animal and not human. The red stone at the heart of the amulet began to glow, then projected a beam of startlingly red light straight up to the heavens. Absently, Darcy noted that all the creatures of the night had ceased making noise; the woods were silent as a grave.

The light widened and began to take shape, losing its glow as it transformed itself into a humanoid creature. But nobody would mistake it for anything natural. It was the approximate size of a human, but its face had only gaping holes where eyes and mouth should be—a truly horrible sight. The creature's hands were skeletal and tipped with claws; they disappeared into grayish-blue wisps of cloth that served as its body. It had no legs but floated a few feet from the ground in the center of the circle. The creature itself made no noise, but the rough cloth that made up its body constantly fluttered in a nonexistent breeze, creating a rustling noise like the wings of several bats.

Darcy shuddered. The leader had summoned a wight.

He had not wanted to credit Tolliver's assertion, but the group's leader was a necromancer, someone who had warped his natural magic until it had the capacity to control the dead. He had made a human ghost corporeal, sundered the soul from God, and enslaved it to his own will. It was an abomination, an affront to every sense of human decency.

Several of the robed watchers flinched away from the creature. Darcy could hardly blame them. Even from his hiding place, Darcy could sense that the thing exuded a horrible sense of despair and hopelessness. As terrible as the creature was, he could still muster sympathy for it; it did not desire to exist in this enslaved state.

6

"You stand in awe of my abilities!" The necromancer gloated, moving to the center of the circle beside his creation. "But you do not know the full extent of my power. I have already created several of these, my servants, and have them hidden as they await my pleasure." Darcy wondered if that was true or if the man was bragging to impress the others.

"Now, for a demonstration of the wight's capabilities!" The necromancer gave a sharp nod to two robed men on his right side. Without warning, they seized Tolliver from among the gathered followers and dragged him toward the necromancer.

"What? Release me!" Tolliver shouted.

"This one sought to betray us!" The necromancer announced to his followers. "He took money and gave information to our enemies." Tolliver babbled about his innocence and devotion to the cause, but nobody was listening.

Darcy's heart pounded. Did the necromancer know what Tolliver had told Darcy? Did they know of Darcy's presence? Or was Tolliver selling information to more than one person? The man was a weasel; Darcy would not be surprised.

Still, nobody deserved the fate that awaited Tolliver. But there were simply too many people surrounding him; Darcy could not manage a rescue. The captive made an inarticulate anguished cry.

"Behold, the fate of traitors!" The necromancer gestured grandly to the wight, which glided toward the prisoner. It enveloped him and fastened its mouth to his neck. Tolliver screamed, an unearthly wail of despair as if his soul were being sucked from his body. His body went limp. The wight released it and it fell to the ground with a dull thud.

The necromancer raised his arms triumphantly. "This is the power of a single wight! Soon I will have an army of them!"

The words sent horrified shivers down Darcy's back. *What was the necromancer scheming to do with an army of wights?*

Another follower brought forth a metal box, somewhat like a safe. Using chants and gestures, the necromancer forced the wight into the box, far too small to accommodate the creature, but it was a type of ghost after all. Once the wight was safely stowed, the necromancer lowered his arms, looking exhausted. "It is done."

This signaled the end of the ritual. The fire died down and the robed figures broke their formation. Some removed their robes, talking softly with their compatriots. A few of the followers made furtive glances at Tolliver's body—a graphic warning against betraying their leader.

Nobody was paying any attention to the amulet lying on the blood-soaked rock.

Darcy took a deep breath, endeavoring to slow his racing heart. The events he had observed in the clearing were far more dangerous and disturbing than Richard had feared when he had first heard rumors of the group. Darcy would need to convey this information to the Assessor's Agency immediately; a threat of this size would need to be handled by Director Cranston in consultation with the Council for Enchantment.

But if Darcy could obtain the amulet, the director might glean some clues about the necromancer's activities—perhaps even his identity. It would also prevent the blackguard from creating more wights.

Darcy swathed himself in shadows and crept into the clearing, watching the mancers talk and even joke. If he had not just observed them participating in a dark magic ritual and murder, he would have thought they were meeting at White's Gentleman's Club. The necromancer was completely surrounded by sycophantic followers. He and many of the other mancers kept their masks on, so Darcy could not identify them.

Their voices were loud enough to cover any noises Darcy made. Staying low to the ground, he raced to the tall rock and grabbed the amulet. Unfortunately, Fletchley happened to be glancing in that direction. He could not see Darcy, covered in shadows, but he glimpsed the amulet moving through the air until Darcy slung it around his neck and concealed it again.

"The amulet! Where is the amulet? Someone is stealing it!" Fletchley shouted.

Abandoning all thoughts of silence, Darcy crashed through the underbrush at the far edge of the clearing. Shadows continued to conceal him, but the sounds of his passage would allow them to pursue him.

He ran for the river and the trees and brambles lining its banks. Crashes and shouts suggested his pursuers were not far behind. Apparently one of the pursuers was an illuminomancer, who pulled light from the moon to illuminate the whole area. It did nothing to pierce Darcy's shadows, but it allowed the pursuers to follow the path of broken twigs and crushed vegetation in his wake.

Perhaps he should have thought of an escape route before impulsively grabbing the amulet. The horror of Tolliver's death had shaken Darcy more than he had realized.

Up ahead, a tangle of vegetation marked the bank of the River Lea. He had the vague idea that he might be able to escape into the river. He did not know if he was a strong enough swimmer to reach the other bank, but perhaps he could let the current pull him downstream from his pursuers. It was a desperate hope, but Darcy was rather desperate.

He was not far from the river when he tripped over a fallen branch. Damnation! His ankle twisted and he hit his head painfully on a tree root. Momentarily, everything went black. *No! I cannot lose consciousness now. It would mean my death.* He forced his eyes open and struggled to a sitting position. But he had lost control of the concealing shadows when he fell.

"There he is!" With a cry of triumph, one of his pursuers, a tall blond man, leaped upon him and landed a punch on Darcy's jaw. He grabbed for the amulet at Darcy's neck, and Darcy kneed him in the stomach, causing him to fall back.

Fletchley had caught up to them. As Darcy staggered to a standing position, he grabbed Darcy's shirt. "Give us the amulet, and maybe you will live."

Darcy thought of Tolliver's screams. "No."

Fletchley pulled down additional light, shining it directly in his face. "Darcy!"

"Darcy?" the blond said. "From Pemberley? Why is he here?"

Fletchley uttered an oath. "He works for the Assessor's Agency. The leader told me." Darcy wondered how their leader knew such a closely guarded secret.

"The leader definitely doesn't want him carrying stories to them," the blond man said, pulling out a knife.

Darcy drew down shadows, but his attackers were close and had the advantage of Fletchley's illumination. They clearly knew where he was. Darcy backed away, but the blond man closed the distance immediately, slashing out randomly with his knife. Pain slicing across Darcy's ribs told him the blade had found its mark.

Darcy briefly considered fighting, but he was unarmed. Moreover, additional pursuers were on their way to join his attackers. His only hope was to escape.

He gasped in pain as the knife grazed his thigh, but he managed to pull the shadows around him as he ran for the river, his injured ankle protesting each step.

He dared not glance behind him, but his pursuers were so near he could hear their breathing. His only advantage was that the shadows rendered him almost invisible. He dodged around the trunk of a tree and there was the river.

Without hesitation, he dove for the water, aiming to be as far out into the Lea as was possible.

The splash was tremendous, and the shock of cold water made him gasp. It might be summer, but the water was hardly temperate. He stayed under as long as he could, breaking the surface as quietly as possible and then exposing only his head.

Splashes told him that his two pursuers had followed him into the water. Darcy pulled shadows to conceal his head, using only the barest movement to keep himself afloat as the current pulled him downstream. The two men called to each other as Fletchley illuminated wide swathes of the river. But his light could not penetrate Darcy's shadows. The current was sluggish, but the river was moving him away from their position.

Finally Fletchley said, "This is impossible. He could be halfway to London."

"I doubt it," the blond man said. "I got a couple of good cuts in. He's probably sinking to the bottom."

Darcy longed to dispute this assertion, but he was not sure the man was wrong. His head throbbed where he had hit the tree root. When he touched the area gingerly with his fingers, it was bigger than an egg. That could not be good. And he could only imagine how much of his blood was flowing into the river from the two knife wounds. If he were a betting man, Darcy would not give good odds on his survival at the moment.

"And if he lives?" Fletchley asked.

"He has to come ashore some time, and Fitzwilliam Darcy is hardly inconspicuous. We will find him."

Fletchley gave a harsh bark of laughter. "True enough."

Darcy was already many yards away when the men splashed noisily for the riverbank. That danger past, he turned his attention to not drowning—certainly the greatest concern at the moment, he thought muzzily. Possible head contusions and knife wounds would have to wait.

Or perhaps they would not. He closed his eyes against a world that was spinning for reasons that had nothing to do with being in the river. He had no inclination to swim for the bank and was not even sure where it was.

All in all, he thought, these would be excellent conditions in which to drown. He even wondered if that would be such a bad thing. He was so tired; death sounded rather peaceful.

No. I must tell the director of the danger posed by the necromancer and his followers. And I cannot leave Georgiana alone.

When did duty become the only thing of value in my life?

Philosophizing later. Survival now.

Perhaps he could float…But he needed something to help keep him from sinking. He managed to crack open his eyes and searched the nearby area using the limited light provided by the moon. Ah. There was a sturdy-looking log bobbing on the surface. He made his way toward it. Darcy was usually a powerful swimmer, but each stroke was agony as it pulled on the cut across his ribs.

When he reached the log, he wrapped both arms around the top and rested his head on his arms. *Perhaps that will be proof against drowning. If not…well, I did my best.*

Was he imagining a whirlpool or was that the darkness sucking him down?

Chapter Two

"Lizzy, be careful!" Jane Bennet called as her sister Elizabeth shimmied up the pine tree. Today Elizabeth was wearing trousers and intended to take advantage of the freedom they afforded her. She wished she could wear them more often but had promised her mother that she would only wear them around the Bennet family's Longbourn estate.

Elizabeth climbed as high as she could before taking in the view. Most of the land belonged to her family, including a section of the riverbank along the River Lea. A few small fishing boats were visible downstream, but there were no barges or large boats close to Longbourn.

She was about to climb down when she glimpsed a flash of blue mixed in with greens and browns at the edge of the river. Trees and plants always grew in an unruly mess on the riverbank, so it was difficult to distinguish anything clearly. Was it a scrap of fabric? Heavens! It was more than a scrap; it was a sleeve, attached to an arm and a head. Oh no! A dead body.

Then the man's head moved infinitesimally. He was alive!

Elizabeth climbed down as quickly as she dared, unconcerned with sap on her hands or twigs in her hair. As she neared the ground, she called out to her sister. "Jane! Jane! There is a man in the river!"

By the time Elizabeth's feet hit the ground, Jane was already running for the bank, but she was hampered by her long skirts; her younger sister soon overtook her. Elizabeth pushed through the shrubs and brambles that clustered along the river, and Jane followed in her wake. "I believe he was this way." Elizabeth gestured to where she had observed the man. "There he is!"

His head and arms rested on a rotting log while the rest of his body was submerged in the river. Wet hair was plastered to his head, and his eyes were closed. Mud caked his clothing and face. But one of the man's fingers twitched. He was alive.

For now.

If I can retrieve him from the river, I might be able to keep him alive. She burned with the desire to help him. But he was still a good six feet away and undoubtedly weighed more than either woman. Elizabeth turned to her sister, who was yanking on her skirt, which had caught on a branch. "Jane? Can you extract him from the river?" Jane was an aquamancer, a mage gifted with power over water in all its forms.

Jane studied the situation for a moment. "I cannot move him, but I can cause the water to recede." She reached out her hands, extending her magic to the river. Slowly the water drew away from the man, revealing more of his torso lying in the river mud. He was wearing a coat, waistcoat, and breeches. A gentleman then! How curious. Elizabeth had assumed he was a fisherman who had fallen from a boat.

Elizabeth clambered down the muddy bank, thankful she had worn boots, and endeavored to reach the log the man was clinging to, but it was too far. She risked slipping and falling into the river—which would not help anyone.

"Is there any way you can bring him closer?" she asked her sister.

Jane gestured, and a wave formed in the middle of the river, a gentle swell that pushed the man further up the bank.

Hooking her leg around a bush, Elizabeth pulled on the end of the rotting log, attempting to bring him closer. But when the log moved, the man lost his grip, slid backward in the mud, and immediately sank into the river. "Oh no!" Without hesitating, Elizabeth jumped after him. He would not drown if she could save him. Fortunately, the water was shallow this close to the bank and she could stand.

It was murky, and she had to root around with her hands to find the man's body. She brushed against an arm. Wrapping her fingers around it, she reached around for the other arm and pulled his torso from the water. The man's head hung slack, and he did not appear to be breathing. Elizabeth was panting, her muscles protesting the unaccustomed exercise. *How can I possibly remove him from the river?*

Suddenly he was buoyed from underneath, floating quite lightly on the surface. Elizabeth did not know how Jane had managed such a feat. "Oh! Well done!" she called to her sister. Now it was just a matter of tugging the man to the riverbank.

She propped him up, noticing the grayish pallor of his skin. "Oh no," she told the strange man. "I did not undergo all this trouble for you to perish now." She sent her awareness into his body, willing his lungs to fulfill the function they were designed to do. The barest hint of breath trickled out of his mouth. She sent more energy into the man's lungs. He inhaled, a slight flaring of his nostrils. *Good. That would do for the moment.*

Getting her feet underneath her in the mud of the riverbank, she held the man around his waist and called up to Jane. "Can you help us to land?"

"Yes. I think I understand this now."

A wave, almost like a giant hand, pushed the man gently upward until Jane could grab under his arms. She pulled while Elizabeth pushed the man's legs. She attempted to ignore the impropriety of the situation; her mother would be appalled. Thank heavens the man was insensible! Together they lifted him onto dry land. Elizabeth pulled herself out after him, dripping water and covered in mud.

Jane held him under his arms, and Elizabeth held his feet as they carried him through the brambles at the river's edge to a patch of grass just beyond. Even with two of them, it was a struggle. He was tall and sodden, a dead weight in their arms.

As they laid him gently on the grass, Jane inquired, "Can you save him?"

"I hope so." Elizabeth *had* managed to restore his breathing, but the truth was she had never attempted to heal anyone this far gone. When she was summoned for a healing, it was usually for a broken bone or similar accident. She could ease pain for naturally occurring illnesses, but she could not heal them. Assisting a drowning victim was something she had never faced. And God knew what else might be troubling him.

But surely the first task was to help him breathe without her assistance.

She extended her magic, sensing the spark of life in his body. "He lives – at least at the moment," she told Jane. "But his lungs are full of water. Can you expel the water from his body?"

Jane's lips thinned into a white line. "I have never commanded water inside a human body. But I can make the attempt." She stared fiercely at the man, no doubt using her magical senses to identify the river water in the man's lungs.

"Turn him on his side," Jane ordered. Elizabeth tugged on the man's shoulders until he was lying on his side.

Jane gestured with quick, sharp strokes. Water started trickling out of the man's mouth and then gushed as the man coughed. When it was all expelled, the man coughed wetly and started breathing with terrible rasping breaths.

Elizabeth rolled him to his back and skimmed her hands a few inches above his body, searching for those places where his life energies were not flowing freely. In fact, energy was leaking out of his body in two different places. She pulled aside his shirt and the bottom edge of his waistcoat to reveal a deep gash along his ribs. Jane gasped at the blood oozing from the wound. "He was stabbed?"

"Yes. This is not a matter of someone who simply fell out of a boat."

Sensing more trouble, she found a rip along the left leg of his breeches, revealing a long, shallow knife cut. Jane gasped.

"Someone did not care for this fellow." Elizabeth endeavored to keep her voice level, but the evidence of violence was disturbing.

Energy was knotted at the back of his head. When she probed the area with her fingers, he winced. "A contusion from a blow to the head," she reported to Jane. "He also sustained some damage to his ankle, but he will not be needing to walk for a while yet."

"He is fortunate to still be alive," Jane remarked. "Can you help him?"

Elizabeth took a deep breath. "I think so. I cannot heal everything today, but I believe I can repair the worst damage."

She pushed her hand through layers of coat and shirt so she could touch his flesh. This sort of deep healing would not work without direct contact with his skin. At least he was unconscious; it would be mortifying to touch a man who was awake! The muscle and tissue longed to be whole again. She could almost hear the flesh crying out at the violation created by the two slices of the knife. She sank her awareness into the layers of muscle, fat, and tissue, carefully encouraging it to knit back together.

Fortunately, the ribs had prevented the knife from penetrating further into the chest. And the slice on the leg was shallow. However, she did not know how much blood the man had lost or if he might contract an infection.

Next, she healed the lung tissues damaged by water and eased the swelling at the back of his head. Customarily she drew on the patient's body to fuel such healing, but the man's energy was already vastly depleted. She was forced to draw on her own, and even so, she could not fix everything. The stab wounds would be well on their way to healing, but she could not cause them to disappear.

Exhausted, she slumped backward, landing on her bottom in the grass. How long had she been healing? She often lost track of time in a healing trance. The sun was lower in the sky. It must have been an hour or more.

A hand clasped under her elbow and helped her to stand. Her father. Jane must have fetched him while Elizabeth was busy performing the healing. "Are you well, Lizzy?" he asked.

She leaned against him for a moment, taking pleasure in his warmth. Her damp clothing caused her to be cold and clammy. "Yes, Papa, just tired. I do not believe I have ever healed someone so close to death."

"You did well. He is breathing easily, and his color has improved even since I arrived."

"How long have you been here?"

"Not above half an hour." Only then did Elizabeth notice that her father was accompanied by Tom, a burly footman, and a cart that was often used on the farm. That would allow them to transport the stranger more easily. Her father examined him. "I wonder how he came to be in the river. He appears to be a gentleman."

Elizabeth really scrutinized her patient for the first time. His clothing was of fine quality and very well cut, obviously tailored specifically for him. His cravat was missing as were his boots. His clothes were sodden and muddy. But the man had begun his day as well-dressed as any gentleman Elizabeth had ever met.

The man was tall and well-built. He was younger than she had first thought, no more than thirty. Dark hair curled around his head. His features were fine and patrician, a Roman god come to life. What color would his eyes be? If Elizabeth had encountered him at a house party or a dance, she would have given him a second glance. She would not have minded catching his eye.

Not that she ever caught anyone's eye.

"We should take him to the manor and a room with a fire," her father said. "And you need to remove your wet clothing."

The reminder made Elizabeth shiver. "Yes, he should not be exposed to the elements any more than necessary." She took a step toward the house, but the world went gray and tilted. Her father caught her with a hand around her waist. "I think you must sit down for a bit, my dear. You have exerted a lot of energy on this gentleman's behalf."

Elizabeth nodded wearily and sank back down on the grass. At least her clothing could not become any muddier.

Tom brought the cart around. He and her father gently lifted the man into it, cushioning him on a bed of hay. Tom tugged the cart back to the road, where he had a donkey to pull it back to the manor. Papa helped

Elizabeth to stand. They followed at a slow pace as she leaned on his strength.

Soon Longbourn Manor came into view. It was one of the oldest houses in Hertfordshire, built of gray stone that was—truth be told—crumbling in some places. Ivy clung to the walls no matter how frequently Elizabeth encouraged it to grow elsewhere. Elizabeth's mother complained that the house was old, drafty, and dark. However, Kitty, who read a great many novels, insisted that Longbourn was Gothic and mysterious.

But mysterious was the theme for the day as they brought a mysterious gentleman into their midst. What was such a man doing in the river? How had he sustained those injuries? It was very intriguing. No doubt her entire family would be interested in the mystery.

***

Fitzwilliam Darcy opened his eyes. A woman's face filled his field of vision. Dark curls and blue-green eyes. She hovered over him, regarding him with concern. Noticing his attention, she quickly withdrew, giving him a shy smile.

How beautiful. Those were lips I would love to kiss. Would she let me kiss her? I hope so. But perhaps I should not. I do not know her name. It would be wrong to kiss a woman whose name I do not know.

"How are you feeling?" The words seemed to come from very far away.

Exhaustion dragged him down into darkness once more. He desired to stay and talk to her—tell her how her face delighted him. "Beautiful..." he mumbled.

She laughed and started to speak again. But Darcy had already slipped into the darkness.

***

Darcy was aware of moving between periods of waking and sleeping, unsure of what was real and what was a dream. When his eyes finally opened, Darcy was more alert. He noted some details of his surroundings: a wholly unfamiliar room with blue striped wallpaper and well-made but worn oak furniture. The chamber was bathed in lemony yellow sunlight from two open windows that were framed by lacy curtains blowing in the breeze.

Awaking in a strange room should have been frightening, or at least disconcerting. However, Darcy found it difficult to experience anything other than pleasure that he was alive. He had no idea how he had arrived at this place, but he had expected to awaken cold, wet, and in pain. He could not possibly object to his situation. Surely nothing terrible threatened Darcy in such a room. He could not imagine that the necromancer decorated his house in blue stripes and lace.

Endeavoring to sit up provoked the discovery that Darcy was strong enough to only lift his head, but he could survey the room. Only then did he realize he was not alone.

A dark-haired young woman was laying down a book and uncurling herself from a chair in the far corner. She was familiar from his intermittent periods of semi-alertness.

A maid assigned to watch over the patient? No, her dress was too fine; she must be a gentlewoman. What was she doing alone with him? Perhaps she was married. Although if Darcy had a wife that pretty, he would not have left her alone with a strange young man. *On the other hand, I am not much of a threat to her virtue.*

She crossed to his bedside. "Would you like some water?"

Following his nod, she held a glass and supported his head while he drank eagerly. Nothing had ever tasted as good as that tepid water. Exhausted from that slight exertion, Darcy allowed his head to sink gratefully onto the pillow while she returned the empty glass to the bedside table.

"How are you feeling?" she asked in a soft voice—so rich it was almost musical to Darcy's ears.

"Where—" He coughed and cleared his throat. "Where am I?"

"Hertfordshire."

Hertfordshire? He had never been in that part of the country. "How— How far from Luton?"

Her eyebrows shot upward. "Is that where you were? We are quite a ways."

What had happened while Darcy was insensible? How long ago had he fallen in the river? What had Richard thought when Darcy had not reported in? He yearned to leap from the bed and order a carriage for London, but he was patently incapable of travel.

The people in this house had taken care of him, kept him alive. But could he trust them? He felt for the amulet on its chain around his neck. Thank God it was still there. Surely if they were in league with the necromancer, they would have deprived him of it already. Still, he needed to be careful.

The woman had noticed the gesture. "Yes, we left the amulet around your neck. You are fortunate not to have lost it in the river. A curious object. I believe it may have some magical properties."

Darcy stilled, but her manner was open and unaffected, showing only a passing interest in the item. "Yes, it has some slight magic," he said slowly. "A family heirloom…I am pleased it was not lost."

She nodded briskly. "Will you tell me your name?" the woman asked.

"D—" Darcy stopped himself. The enemy would be searching for him. "You can call me…William."

She chuckled, a low and lovely sound. "Surely I cannot be so informal! For all that you are in my home, we have not actually been introduced." Playfulness in her tone suggested she took the dictates of propriety rather less seriously than Darcy did. What kind of a woman was she?

"I am Mr. D."

"Mr. Dee?" She gave him a quick, ironic curtsey. "I am pleased to meet you. I am Elizabeth Bennet, and you are a guest in my family's home of Longbourn."

She was altogether charming. Many other women would have peppered him with questions, retreated into shyness, or fussed about his health. Her directness was refreshing, helping him bear his current weakness. "I must thank you for your hospitality," he said formally.

"It is our pleasure. Is there anyone we should contact on your behalf? Where is your family?"

"I have a house in London." That was true enough. "My family raises sheep and sells wool." That was also true; Pemberley had a lively wool trade, although it was hardly the chief source of income. Thoughts of home recalled Darcy to his duty. "I should send a note to my cousin…." However, the mere thought of attempting to write was exhausting.

"Perhaps when you are improved," Miss Bennet suggested. He must have appeared as tired as he felt.

"How long have I been asleep?"

"More than a day. You arrived here yesterday morning, and it is now evening."

As long as that? Richard must be frantic with worry. Fortunately, Georgiana was at Matlock with family and believed Darcy to be in town.

Richard would write her a letter to account for Darcy's lack of correspondence. "Arrived? How did I arrive?" The last thing Darcy recalled was diving into the river with the expectation that he would drown.

"Via a most unconventional means. You were traveling in the River Lea without a boat, which does not have much to recommend itself by way of transportation. My sister and I found you along the riverbank."

Darcy was amazed at his good fortune. He had a vague recollection of being pulled out of the water but regarded her skeptically. "You and your sister pulled me out of the river? Perhaps with the help of your husband?"

She regarded him blankly. "I am unmarried, sir. My sister and I took you from the river with some effort. My father and a footman transported you here." Perhaps she was unaware of how much she revealed. Not only was she unwed, but her family was wealthy enough to keep a manservant.

"Your father allows you to be in a bedchamber with an unknown man?"

To his amazement, she laughed. "You are hardly in a position to do me harm. Even if you managed to stand, I could easily push you over."

He coughed, imagining that he still had river water in his lungs. "All too true, I am afraid. But propriety…." Clearly this was a family wealthy enough to care for the reputation of an unwed daughter.

She leaned forward and spoke in a low voice. "I shall not tell anyone if you do not."

Darcy found himself smiling despite the circumstances.

"Do you wish me to leave?" she asked.

"No," he said hastily and found he meant it. Apparently recovering from a near-death experience was far more pleasant if one had company. "I enjoy your conversation."

She did not simper and blush as he expected. Instead, she gave him a look of mock disapproval. "Now, sir, you are not yet strong enough to expend energy upon compliments to a lady. Conserve your strength."

This elicited a chuckle from him. "It was not intended as a compliment; it was simply the truth."

Now a faint blush did stain her cheek, and she averted her eyes. "Are you in pain?"

He attempted to sit up in bed and was rewarded with an ache in his side. *Oh yes. I was stabbed.* Touching the skin over his ribs, he discovered that the area was covered by a bandage, but the pain was not nearly as sharp as he expected.

"That wound and the one in your leg are mostly healed, but there is still a chance you may develop an infection," Miss Bennet said.

"Mostly healed?" How was that possible? It had only been two days.

"We did what we could to heal them and reduce the swelling from the blow to your head and the ankle injury. But everything will require additional time and rest."

Darcy gingerly touched the bump on the back of his head, wincing at even light contact. And how did she even know that his ankle was injured? Surely he had not attempted to walk?

"How long does the doctor suppose I must remain in bed?" he asked.

"The doctor has not examined you."

No doctor? The thought alarmed Darcy. "Who treated me then?"

"I did." Miss Bennet colored slightly. "I have a bit of healing magic."

Oh. A few puzzle pieces fell into place. Magical healers were rare outside of large cities. Darcy had been exceedingly fortunate indeed. No doubt she was being modest, and she was the reason for his unexpected survival. "Did you train in London?"

She cast her eyes down. "No. I have only visited London twice."

Twice? When they live so close? Her family might have limited means, but such isolation was odd.

"My family does not travel extensively," she added. "When you are healed, I hope you will tell me about the places you have visited." He recognized the hunger for knowledge in her eyes. He possessed such hunger as well but was fortunate to have the means to indulge it.

"Of course," he said. "It is the least I can do to thank you for your efforts on my behalf." She had saved his life. He would need to find a more substantial way to repay that debt.

"We can send for the doctor if you wish," Miss Bennet said.

"That is not necessary. I believe your care has been quite beneficial."

She wagged a finger at him. "Now you are wasting strength on compliments once again!"

He laughed. Did he dare to suppose she found him amusing—even charming? He never had much luck with charming women. *Not that I wish to charm her*, he reminded himself sternly. Although she was witty and quite lovely, her family would not mingle with Darcy's level of society. Naturally, her attentions to him were because he was her patient; she wanted him to recover.

"Pray tell me how a wool merchant found himself in the River Lea," she said.

He blinked. He had not said he was a wool merchant, but it was as good a story as any. Darcy was tantalized by the idea that the home's inhabitants would not know about his identity, income, or lands in Derbyshire. While at Longbourn, he could shed the expectations of the *ton*.

Many merchants traveled extensively to find new markets for their wares, so it accounted for his presence in Luton. "I was set upon by highwaymen and dove into the river to escape. I did not expect to awake here." Belatedly, Darcy wondered where his watch and money purse were. Probably at the bottom of the river with his boots—he could vaguely recall removing them when they filled with water. At least it lent credence to his story.

She stared at him aghast. "That is terrible! You are fortunate you survived!"

"Indeed. Thanks to your family's care." He reached out to touch her wrist. "But I pray you…please prevail upon your family not to speak of my presence here. There will be…men looking for me. They are the ones who gave me this." He gestured to the knife wound.

She frowned. "But surely you have nothing they could be in want of."

Darcy endeavored to think through the muddle in his mind as exhaustion crept up on him. "The situation is complex….They have a grudge against my family…." The lie sounded thin to his ears. He had grown more accustomed to deception during his two years working with the Agency, but he was never comfortable with it. He preferred sneaking around in the dark. "It is vitally important that it remain a secret." He yearned to sound firm, but his voice was weakening.

Miss Bennet nodded. "Nobody knows you are here, save my family and our servants. I will request their discretion. We have only limited intercourse with the rest of Hertfordshire in any event."

Why was that? But Darcy's eyelids were growing heavy; he did not have the energy to inquire.

She stood. "I believe you require additional rest. Perhaps we can prepare some tea and broth for you the next time you awaken."

"I am not hungry at this moment, but perhaps if I sleep a little, I might be…." His last thought was to curse the weakness of his body as he tumbled into darkness.

Chapter Three

Elizabeth shut the door to Mr. Dee's room and descended the stairs to the blue sitting room which was full of Bennet family members. Everyone glanced up when she entered.

"I heard your voice. Is our mysterious guest awake?" her father inquired.

"He was awake enough to answer some questions," Elizabeth responded. "And he drank some water, but he is sleeping again."

"Is he civil?" Jane asked.

"Is he married?" Lydia asked.

"Is he wealthy?" her mother asked.

Elizabeth laughed. "Yes he is civil. He did not mention a wife. And I did not think to inquire about the exact amount of his family's fortune, but they are wool merchants with a house in town."

"In trade?" Elizabeth's sister Mary wrinkled her nose.

"Pssh! Who cares where the money comes from?" her mother said. "Wool...." She sighed. "Everyone needs wool. A wool merchant would do very well for one of you."

"Mama, men who have been rescued from the river are not necessarily in want of a wife," Elizabeth noted.

Her mother only jabbed her embroidery more energetically. "We must not waste such an opportunity! He might take a liking to one of you girls."

"He has requested that we tell no-one of his whereabouts," Elizabeth told her father.

"Ooo! Perhaps he is an escaped prisoner!" Kitty said, sounding quite excited at the prospect. She read a lot of novels.

"I do not believe prisoners customarily wear such fine clothing," Elizabeth said.

"A French soldier in hiding?" Kitty guessed.

"He has no accent," Elizabeth said.

"A viscount who is secretly also a highwayman!"

"They are not as plentiful as you have been led to believe," Elizabeth said with a smile.

"Perhaps he is—" Kitty started.

"Perhaps he is a wool merchant, and we should not let our imaginations run wild," Elizabeth said firmly.

"His desire for secrecy is quite interesting," her father remarked. "I was in Clark's book shop today when a stranger inquired if anyone had reported a body washing up along the river. He said his brother had fallen in the river near Luton."

"Surely it cannot be the same man," Jane exclaimed. "Mr. Dee could not have floated all the way from Luton." Elizabeth said nothing.

Her father shrugged. "I agree it is improbable. But it is almost equally improbable to fish a stranger from the river at the same moment someone is seeking another fellow."

"You did not say anything about Mr. Dee?" Elizabeth asked anxiously.

Her father snorted. "I would not share any news with Clark that I would not care to have spread about the entire county. A strange man staying in my house with my five unmarried daughters is not such a thing."

"Perhaps Mr. Dee's family is searching for him," Jane said, her forehead creased with worry.

Elizabeth shook her head. "Mr. Dee knows how to contact his family. We should not reveal anything without consulting him."

"I agree. Mr. Dee should decide who knows his whereabouts. He may have reason to be careful. Perhaps they are waging a vicious war with the cotton merchants." Her father laughed at his own joke.

"Perhaps he is a viscount disguised as a wool merchant!" Kitty suggested.

"Whatever else he is, we know he is an injured man who needs to recover his strength," Elizabeth said. "We must leave him in peace to do so."

"Can't I at least tell Maria Lucas?" Lydia inquired. "'Tis the most interesting thing that has happened in months! I will swear her to secrecy."

Her father fixed her with a stern gaze. "No, you may not."

Lydia huffed and rolled her eyes. "Very well. I will add it to the list of subjects I may not speak about."

"I don't know why you bother befriending anyone in Meryton," Mary said with a sniff. "They are quite unpleasant."

"I don't know why I bother either," Lydia whined. "Nobody likes us." She stood and flounced out of the room.

Of the five sisters, Lydia suffered the most from Longbourn's relative isolation from the rest of Hertfordshire. Mary spent her time with religious books, and Kitty was absorbed in novels. Jane and Elizabeth spent much time honing their magical skills. But Lydia longed to be just like all the other girls in the neighborhood, and their mother indulged those desires. The Lucases at least would allow their daughters to socialize with the Bennet girls; Lydia took full advantage of those privileges.

Kitty shrugged. "They are pleased with us when they have need of our assistance." She returned to her novel.

Sadly, this was true. How many times had Jane helped farmers with flooded fields or prevented someone's house from being swept away? The people of Meryton never hesitated to call upon Kitty when a wildfire threatened houses or crops. And Elizabeth had healed many people in the neighborhood.

Yet their talents set them apart. Mancy was rare outside London, but it was rampant in the Bennet family. When they walked into Meryton, people stared and spoke behind their hands. They even made signs to avert the evil eye.

Papa compounded the problem. He never particularly cared about the neighbors' opinions and at times relished his reputation for eccentricity. At public occasions, he would tell odd jokes without any concern about how it might affect the family name. Her mother frequently lamented that no man in the neighborhood would ever consider courting a Bennet girl.

Mary often said the townspeople did not deserve their help if they ostracized the family. Elizabeth understood her sister's frustration, but she would never refuse someone in need. Mary closed her book of sermons and turned to their father. "If we always help them in their time of need, we should at least collect money for our services."

Her father sighed. "We have no need to rehearse that argument. *We* are not in trade." He stood and ambled toward the door. "Lizzy, I will be in my study should our guest wish to speak with me."

***

When Darcy awoke the next morning, he was hungry and more alert. He was also alone in the room. To his amazement, the bell by his bedside did not summon a servant but Miss Elizabeth.

Darcy was embarrassed. "I had not intended to call for you. I merely hoped to break my fast."

She shrugged, unperturbed. "I must learn how you are healing." She sat beside his bed without any apparent concerns for modesty and spread her hands over his head. It was rather disconcerting. He had never encountered a female healer before, and Miss Elizabeth was quite attractive with her dark curls and blue-green eyes. His body was quite aware of her proximity.

"I believe the lump on your head has diminished," she said after a moment.

Darcy did not consider himself an overly modest person, but would she wish to examine the cut along his ribs? No doubt she had viewed his chest when he was unconscious. However, his body was sufficiently recovered that it might now react in noticeable ways.

Fortunately, she merely skimmed her hands a few inches over his body. "Your cuts are healing well, but I have noticed signs that may be incipient infection," she reported.

"Can you heal it?"

She shook her head. "I can ease some of the symptoms of infection, but I cannot prevent infection itself. My mancy does not function in that way. I pray you do not fail to rest."

"I will not," he promised.

She stood to retreat, but the door flew open and a younger girl bounced in, apparently heedless of the propriety of entering a strange man's room. She was taller than Miss Elizabeth, but not nearly as pretty despite her blonde curls.

"Mama needs you," she informed her sister. Her eyes darted to the bed. "Ooo! The mysterious stranger is awake."

Miss Elizabeth gave her a quelling look. "This is Mr. Dee. Mr. Dee, this is my sister Catherine, or Kitty."

"How do you do?" he said.

She stared at Darcy for a long moment. He supposed strangers in this area were uncommon. But she finally remembered to give him a curtsey. "Pleased to meet you."

"Kitty is the second youngest of my sisters," Miss Elizabeth remarked.

"How many sisters do you have?" he asked.

"There are five of us," Miss Kitty responded.

"We should let Mr. Dee rest," Miss Elizabeth said, opening the door again. However, another girl— who had obviously been eavesdropping—fell into the room.

Miss Elizabeth rolled her eyes. "This is Lydia, my youngest sister. Lydia, this is Mr. Dee."

"You said you would tell us when he awoke!" Miss Lydia exclaimed.

"I said I would tell you when he was ready for company. He is not," Miss Elizabeth said.

Miss Kitty regarded her sister. "Did he reveal why he was in the river? Is he a pirate?"

Miss Elizabeth gave Darcy an ironic smile. "Please forgive my sisters. They have active imaginations." She shooed her sisters toward the door. "Mr. Dee needs to rest."

"Not a pirate?" Miss Kitty asked.

"I am afraid not," Darcy said, thanking providence that they had not thought to inquire if he was a spy.

The girls pouted, disappointed about his plebian occupation. "I do not believe pirates ply their trade on the Lea," Elizabeth murmured.

"What about a lost duke?" Miss Kitty inquired eagerly.

"No."

"A prince?"

"No."

"Then who are you?"

Miss Elizabeth laughed. "Are those the only available options? Pirate, prince, or duke?"

"I am just a wool merchant," Darcy said, hoping he appeared uninteresting.

The younger sisters exchanged disappointed looks. "That is not particularly mysterious," Miss Lydia complained.

"Oddly enough," Miss Elizabeth said. "I do not suppose Mr. Dee fell into the river for your amusement." Her sisters looked unhappy, so she finally relented and said, "However, he *was* set upon by highwaymen."

Two sets of eyes went wide. "Did they say, 'Stand and deliver'?" Miss Kitty asked.

He shook his head. "They were not so polite."

"You may hear the whole story some other time—when Mr. Dee is feeling better." Miss Elizabeth finally managed to chivvy the girls out the door. She turned to him. "I apologize for my sisters' ill manners. Are you well enough to eat?"

He nodded. "I am quite hungry."

"I will send up a tray. I would recommend mostly broth and tea today, but if that agrees with you, we might try some bread later."

He was resigned to his fate. "I understand." He did not want her to quit the room and could imagine any number of methods for prolonging her visit. But he was being ridiculous. He must simply be as starved for human companionship as he was for food.

"Please ring if you need anything." Elizabeth closed the door firmly behind her.

***

By late afternoon Mr. Dee had developed the infection Elizabeth had predicted. Every time she visited his chamber, he was sleeping restlessly. She used cold compresses to bring down the fever and attempted to rouse him to drink willow bark tea. Her healing powers reduced the effects of the fever and accompanying aches, but they could do nothing about the underlying illness. Her healing mancy was also depleted from previous usage and she had less energy for the task than she would prefer. Fortunately, the fever did not appear to be extremely high, and he slept peacefully.

That evening, before retiring to bed, Elizabeth slipped out the backdoor to admire the moon and the stars—a common habit when the weather was fair. It was an exceptionally clear night, and the moon was full overhead, casting a pale gray light over everything. Frogs and crickets chirped, the soothing sounds of a summer night. Closing her eyes, she took pleasure in the cool refreshing breeze blowing over her face.

It took her a moment to recognize what had changed. The world had gone silent. The crickets. The frogs. All the creatures of the night had fallen silent in one instant. How bizarre. What could be the cause?

She looked around but perceived nothing amiss. Still, the back of her neck prickled uneasily.

Then she heard a strange rustling noise. At first, it sounded far away but then it grew louder. Almost as if someone moved in a stiff taffeta gown. But the sound emanated from the sky, which made no sense. Glancing up, she caught a glimpse of a grayish shadow from the corner of her eye, but when she turned her head, it was gone. She froze in place, all of her senses alert. Nothing.

But the sound erupted again, much louder, to her right. An ominous rustling noise. The wings of a bat? Or several bats? No. The thing she glimpsed was far too big for a bat. She might have called it a ghost, but ghosts were silent, were they not? Her eyes strained in the darkness, but she saw nothing.

Why am I standing outside in the dark? She usually felt safe on Longbourn's property, but now she imagined how small and defenseless she would appear to a predator in the air.

The rustling sounds grew closer as if the creature was descending, stooping to attack her. Instinctively, she reached with her mind as she would touch a rabbit or deer. But there was nothing of the warm simplicity of an animal consciousness. This creature had an alien blankness where its mind should be—nothing but cold emptiness and an accompanying sense of great dread.

Definitely not a bat.

Chapter Four

That realization, more than anything, pushed her into action. Her mind screamed that she must run. Her legs propelled her toward the house, although she could not perceive if anything pursued her. She pushed through the door and slammed it closed behind her—bolting it for good measure. Her father's wards enveloped her like a warm bath. They were designed to prevent sinister magical beings from entering the house.

Gasping for air, Elizabeth listened at the door but heard and sensed nothing. The rustling creature appeared to have retreated. Thank God!

She sank to the floor on wobbly legs, allowing her heart rate to return to normal. Finally she was able to stand and stumble her way to her bed chamber. Her father was abed already, but she resolved to tell him of the encounter in the morning. Perhaps he would know what the creature might be. For her part, Elizabeth would prefer to forget about it.

***

Darcy awoke to the sound of someone slipping into the room bathed in late afternoon light. "Shh." Miss Elizabeth's voice came from the shadows. "Return to sleep." His eyelids were heavy, and he could not rouse himself despite the desire to speak with her. As he slipped back into his dreams, he thought her hands touched his bandaged side as warmth seeped through his skin. Was that her healing touch? He longed to ask but soon drifted away again.

He could not have said how long he lay in that state, waking infrequently and only rousing himself to drink. Sometimes Miss Elizabeth would be by his bedside, and sometimes it would be a maid applying cool cloths to his forehead. The wound in his side was inflamed and ached to the touch. The one on his leg twinged when he moved the limb. His sheets were soaked with perspiration, and he alternated between too hot and too cold.

In his more lucid moments, Darcy guessed that he had a fever. Other times he dreamt of Pemberley. Of a wight devouring a human body. Of Richard searching for him in the woods. Of Georgiana sobbing. Of a pair of blue-green eyes. Then he slept.

***

Finally, Darcy was alert enough to request tea and broth. Elizabeth arrived immediately behind the maid bearing the tray. "You gave us quite a fright," she told him.

"I apologize for the imposition. How long was I ill?"

"Three days. Do not apologize. I am only pleased you recovered in good time."

I have now been missing for nearly five days. Richard would be frantic with worry. And Darcy desperately needed to share what he had learned of the necromancer and his followers. *I should have sent a message the first day, while I was still lucid.*

"Miss Elizabeth—" His voice sounded raspy to his ears. "Might I send a message to my family? They will be worried about me."

"Certainly. I will send for paper and a quill. A footman can post the letter for you." She departed with an admonition to drink liquids and rest.

If Darcy had not been convinced of the necessity for rest, the effort of writing the letter would have convinced him. Aware that the missive might be intercepted, Darcy included few details. He merely related his location and requested help. Although Darcy himself was not capable of traveling, he could give Richard the amulet and the names of the necromancer's followers, at least those he had recognized. The Agency could work to stop him.

One he had sealed the letter for Matlock House and given it to the footman, Darcy rested more easily. No doubt his cousin would ride for Longbourn immediately upon receiving the letter and Darcy could entrust the mission to him.

That night, Darcy took dinner on a tray in his room, relishing the taste of bread and cheese after days of broth. The next morning, he insisted on standing and walking despite Elizabeth's cautions. She allowed the exercise but insisted that he be attended by a footman. Darcy was loath to concede the need for the fellow's presence, but he put a hand on the man's shoulder for balance. Otherwise, he was quite unsteady on his feet. How fortunate none of his friends could witness him reduced to this pitiful state!

The still-healing cut along his ribs ached as he climbed out of bed and protested as he made slow progress along the floor. The cut on his leg pained him even more when he put weight on it. But such aches were the least of his problems.

Every step was a chore because Darcy's body was as weak as a newborn babe's. Moving his head also had a tendency to set the room to spinning. He gritted his teeth, traversing the length of the room by sheer force of will. But those few minutes of exertion exhausted him; he fell into bed and slept for hours.

It was galling to be so weak and constantly fatigued. Darcy had always prided himself on his health and strength. When he indicated as much to Elizabeth, she smiled and said his frustration was likely a sign that he was healing and encouraged him to eat to regain his strength. Darcy grumbled but knew it was good advice.

In the evening, she was kind enough to sit by his bedside and read to him. He was quite enchanted by her low and melodious voice. She had offered him the choice of *Henry V*, Byron's poetry, or a history of ancient Rome. Elizabeth might not know his real name, but she had accurately guessed his tastes in reading material. Darcy had selected Shakespeare but would have been pleased to hear her reading laundry lists.

When he was strong enough, he answered her questions about travel—describing Scotland, Derbyshire, Ramsgate, the Lakes District, and many other places to her great delight. He had seldom met a person who was so fascinated with visiting new and interesting places—and who had traveled to so few of them. He was unsure if lack of funds was responsible for her circumscribed life or if there was another cause.

The next day, he walked upon two separate occasions, each time becoming steadier on his feet. The progress encouraged him, although he kept in mind Elizabeth's admonishment against pushing himself too quickly. Upon the second occasion, he used a cane for balance and ventured out of his room to explore the home's upper hallways, not yet ready to attempt the stairs.

Now that he was healthier, Elizabeth's visits were accompanied by a maid, but he was able to prevail upon her to read to him. The sound of her voice was very soothing, even when she was reading the most lurid passages in *The Mysteries of Udolpho*. When she had wearied of reading, he told her stories about traveling in Kent, Ireland, and Cornwall—always being careful not to reveal too much about his own identity or reasons for traveling.

The following day, he was eager to push himself faster. He had not heard from Richard and was growing quite concerned. He had expected his cousin to appear on Longbourn's doorstep or at least send a reply. The only possible reasons for Richard's silence were not good. Had something happened to Richard? Was there a crisis at the Assessor's Agency? More than anything, Darcy yearned to ride to London, but he would not survive a mile on horseback in his current state.

He could only pray that his letter had simply gone astray. Darcy resolved to send his cousin a message by another means.

With that and other goals in mind, he rose from his bed the next day and slowly donned his clothing, which the servants had thoroughly cleaned. A maid had even mended the rips where the knife had penetrated. Darcy was quite pleased to have escaped the indignities of nightshirts and dressing gowns.

However, as Darcy regarded himself in the mirror to tie a simple knot in his cravat, he was unsatisfied. His garments were shabbier than anything he had ever worn. And his body was beyond gaunt. In a few weeks he might pass as a beggar on the street. He had received a shave from a footman, but his hair was growing shaggy. Worst of all, Darcy's boots had been lost in the river; he would be meeting the entire Bennet family for the first time while forced to make do with slippers. It rankled, but there was nothing for it.

Noting that he intended to venture downstairs, the maid had hastily summoned Elizabeth. She arrived with a frown on her face, but her expression lightened when she saw him sitting by the fireplace. "You look well, Mr. Dee!"

"I am much improved. It would suit me to be introduced to the rest of your family."

She huffed a laugh. "You are accustomed to having your way, are you not? Very well. They are eager to meet you. But pray take your rest when you need it."

"I will."

"It is a pleasant day. My family is enjoying the breezes in the back garden," Elizabeth said.

"That sounds most agreeable." Darcy had been indoors for far too long.

Over the past few days Darcy had concluded that Longbourn operated a bit differently than the homes of most gentry. The servants were shockingly informal with Elizabeth and spoke familiarly about the family, although they certainly seemed pleased with their employment. He heard talk about the Bennet daughters walking at all hours of the day without any escort.

And the family never had visitors. He would expect a house of this stature to receive callers frequently and be an active part of local society, but they appeared to be Hertfordshire's social pariahs. Although it boded well for concealing Darcy's presence, their isolation was puzzling.

Elizabeth hovered by his side as he levered himself out of the chair and shuffled toward the steps. However, he was able to manage with only the assistance of his cane. He had difficulty managing the stairs, holding the railing so he would not fall. But he was determined.

They exited the house through the back door. After being confined indoors for so long, Darcy was pathetically grateful to walk out under the sun again. The sky was immeasurably vast. Had it always been so large? And the green of the plants was almost painfully intense. He had almost forgotten how such things appeared.

The uneven ground in the garden presented a challenge; he was quite winded by the time they greeted the others. Half a dozen chairs had been arranged in a circle at the edge of the garden beneath the spreading boughs of an oak tree. Darcy gratefully sank into one.

Most of the Bennet family was assembled in the chairs, although the two youngest girls were out gathering flowers. Elizabeth affected the introductions. "Mr. Dee, allow me to introduce my parents, Mr. and Mrs. Bennet, and my sisters Jane and Mary."

Jane was quite pretty and as blonde as Elizabeth was dark. Mary had a pinched look about her eyes; she paid more attention to the plants in the garden than to Darcy. Bewhiskered and graying, Mr. Bennet regarded Darcy genially, while the plump Mrs. Bennet displayed the avid interest he had observed all too often in mothers of the *ton*.

"I must thank you for your hospitality," Darcy said to Mr. Bennet.

"Certainly!" the man replied. "We could hardly allow you to drown in the Lea!"

Darcy immediately concluded that Bennet was not the most tactful man he had ever encountered.

Mrs. Bennet leaned forward in her chair. "Pray tell me, is there a Mrs. Dee?"

"No," Darcy said.

"And you are not engaged to be married?"

"No." Darcy understood the calculations behind her questions. She had five unmarried daughters. Her husband was a gentleman, but they lived rather modestly. Darcy imagined he could give the daughters little in the way of dowries.

She took him to be a prosperous wool merchant, which would mean he was a fine—if not brilliant— match for one of their daughters. She did not know how above their touch Darcy truly was. Well, he had dealt with matchmaking mamas before. He could withstand her assault for the length of his tenure at Longbourn.

"And would you say your family lives comfortably?" she asked. Apparently she did not have a subtle bone in her body.

"Yes," he replied.

Was Mrs. Bennet the reason that Elizabeth had been ensconced in his bedchamber unchaperoned? Had she hoped to create intimacy or claim that he had compromised the young woman? Recalling his first reaction to her, Darcy did not find the idea unappealing. She was beautiful and witty, exactly the sort of woman he would desire as a wife.

Unfortunately, the Bennets were beneath him both socially and magically. Although Elizabeth had strong mancy, he doubted anyone else in the family did. Families with strong magical lineages frequented the balls and parties of the *ton*, and most were represented on the Council.

And then there was the matter of what had caused the Bennets to be ostracized from their neighbors. Given how permissive Mr. Bennet was in his supervision of his daughters, Darcy guessed there had been a scandal. Mrs. Bennet might be eager to marry a daughter to a wealthy stranger before he learned the truth.

Fear of entrapment would have caused Darcy anxiety except that Elizabeth had not acted the least bit flirtatious with him. Although she had been polite and friendly, she had not acted the coquette or asked personal questions. It was puzzling and, truthfully, hurt his pride a bit. Given his wealth, he was not accustomed to disinterest from young women. Perhaps she was sweet on another man, a thought that disturbed him for some reason.

Mrs. Bennet never wanted for conversation. "Did you know that Jane pulled you from the river?" The eldest daughter blushed and kept her eyes fixed on the embroidery in her lap. She was pretty enough that she should have many suitors and appeared to be sweet-tempered. But her eyes did not sparkle with Elizabeth's intelligence, and Darcy found himself perversely annoyed. Elizabeth was beautiful in her own right, and any man would be lucky to win her affections. Why was her mother advocating Jane?

"I thought Miss Elizabeth did that," he said.

"Oh, I am sure Lizzy helped." Her mother waved dismissively. "But Jane is an aquamancer."

"Indeed?" Darcy said. How unusual to find two mancers in one country family. "I thank you for helping to rescue me."

Jane blushed again. "I did little. Lizzy truly saved your life."

"Nonsense!" her mother cried. "Lizzy just did a little healing here and there. Mr. Dee would have drowned without your assistance." Darcy expected Elizabeth to protest, but she pressed her lips together and stared uncomfortably at the garden. Perhaps she was accustomed to her mother devaluing her accomplishments and knew that protesting was useless.

"Well, I am exceedingly grateful to have received assistance from both of you," Darcy said diplomatically.

Mary broke the ensuing silence when she addressed Elizabeth. "The rosemary is not growing well, and I need it for the still room."

"Very well. I will look at it." Elizabeth stood.

"Are you a gardener as well as a healer?" Darcy asked.

Everyone went still for a moment. Had he said something wrong? Then Elizabeth shrugged. "I am good with plants." She tromped off into the garden with Mary, leaving Darcy with her parents and Jane.

Mrs. Bennet wasted no time in extolling her eldest daughter's accomplishments and beauty for several minutes—until Kitty and Lydia arrived boasting armfuls of flowers. The Bennets apparently possessed an extraordinarily abundant garden. Lydia talked incessantly about the quantity of flowers, the weather, the rumor of a militia unit to be stationed in Meryton, gossip she had overheard at the milliner's shop, and other subjects that Darcy had difficulty caring about. Her mother, however, followed with avid attention and frequent asides to Darcy about how clever and pretty her youngest daughter was.

Clearly Lydia was Mrs. Bennet's favorite. She hoped Darcy would take an interest in her—with Jane as a runner-up. But Lydia was a mere fifteen years of age; it would be like wooing one of Georgiana's school friends—a ghastly prospect.

At least Jane was out of the school room, but her pretty placidity could not hold a candle to Elizabeth's charms. *What am I thinking? None of these women would be a suitable match for me.* Although their father was a gentleman, his estate was small. And their mother, she had let slip, was the daughter of a mere attorney. Darcy knew that he must marry a woman from the first ranks of society.

In an attempt to change the subject, Darcy remarked to Mr. Bennet about Elizabeth's remarkable healing talent.

"Has she ever been formally apprenticed to a healer?" Darcy inquired. "I would have guessed she had training in town."

Bennet frowned. "No. She has never trained in London."

Darcy's eyebrows shot upward. "It is not so far."

"I am not fond of the place." Bennet's tone of voice indicated the topic was closed.

Darcy could not imagine why it would be a sensitive subject. "I have never heard of anyone healing someone who was half drowned." Not to mention his knife wound and the blow to his head.

"We are fortunate to benefit from her talent," Bennet said in a tone that suggested he would not welcome further discourse.

"You have not told anyone of my presence at Longbourn?" Darcy asked.

Bennet regarded him appraisingly. "Lizzy relayed your request and we have followed it." An unspoken question hung in the air.

Darcy had considered how to explain the need for secrecy. "I believe I was attacked by a rival mercantile family. They would like nothing better than to eliminate the competition under the guise of a common highwaymen attack."

Bennet's brows lifted. "I had not realized the wool trade was so cutthroat."

"It is rougher than most people know," Darcy said, mentally praying for forgiveness for maligning what was probably a completely honorable and benign profession. "There are many miles of riverbank. Our rivals will not suspect I am here as long as they hear no whispers about a stranger at Longbourn."

Bennet nodded, stroking his chin. "I am happy to extend our hospitality for a few days, so long as you do not bring trouble to my door."

"I do not plan to linger. I will depart as soon as I am able," Darcy said. Although, given his current fatigue, that would not be soon enough for his liking. *Damnit, Richard. Where are you?*

"Are you well enough for a turn around the garden?" Bennet asked. "My daughters are justifiably proud of it. I would be remiss if I did not provide a tour."

Darcy stood and gathered his cane. "It would be my pleasure, but I must beg you to walk slowly."

"Of course."

Darcy struggled somewhat on the garden's gravel paths but was able to keep a steady—albeit slow—pace, leaning more than he would have preferred on the cane.

The garden was extensive and robust and had a variety of unusual plants and flowers in every color of the rainbow. How did they manage to have so many flowers bloom at once? And why did all the plants look so healthy? Bennet claimed they did not employ a gardener. He said the whole family tended the garden except for Mrs. Bennet, whose nerves would not withstand insects.

They passed a patch of rosemary that appeared quite robust. Darcy was puzzled why Mary had expressed concern about it. As they rounded the next curve in the path, they came upon Mary and Elizabeth kneeling by a patch of thyme. Elizabeth's hands hovered over the greenery. At first Darcy thought his eyes were deceiving him, but, no, he saw clearly. The plants were increasing visibly in size as he watched. Elizabeth was causing them to grow.

Bennet cleared his throat noisily, and both women startled before hastily rising to their feet.

Darcy's mouth dropped open as the import of what he had observed struck him. "You are a vegemancer as well as a healer?" he asked. Having two talents was exceedingly rare.

It could even be a sign of dark magic like necromancy. Darcy's chest contracted, and he suddenly had trouble breathing.

Chapter Five

Only one panicked thought pushed its way through Darcy's mind. *No. Not her! Not Elizabeth.*

Elizabeth regarded her father guiltily. Mary shrunk backward as if she would prefer to be somewhere else.

"Yes, she—" Bennet started to say when the truth struck Darcy.

"By God! You are a vivomancer!" Vivomancy gave a mage control over all life and living things. Plants, animals, human bodies: anything that was alive was subject to the vivomancer's power. But it was a talent that only appeared once or twice in a generation. Darcy knew of one vivomancer who lived in London and another who resided in Northumberland, but they were both advanced in years.

She nodded, appearing almost relieved that her secret had been revealed.

In the next moment, Darcy doubted his conclusion "But surely I would have heard if another vivomancer had been discovered." Mr. Dee the wool merchant might not have heard such news but Darcy, well acquainted with many members of the Council, certainly would have known. Such a discovery would have been mentioned in the London papers.

"I am indeed a vivomancer," Elizabeth said in a flat voice. Without even a glance in his direction, she reached up to the low-hanging branches of a nearby tree, where she carefully plucked a robin's egg from a nest. Holding it flat in her palm, she focused her attention on the egg. Within seconds the egg cracked, and a squalling baby bird spilled into her hand. Elizabeth had somehow accelerated the hatchling's growth just as she had encouraged the thyme to grow. Gently, she returned the baby bird to the nest with the remaining eggs, where the mother bird scolded her and took the hatchling under her wing.

Darcy gaped. He had never witnessed anything like this. Necromancers had control over death and dead things, but who enjoyed such control over life? "Why did I not know of this?" Darcy asked.

"We have kept it a secret," Bennet said.

His gaze shifted from Elizabeth to her father. "Why?" Vivomancers were sought after and feted. She could help her family become extremely wealthy.

Bennet scowled. "I have no desire for my daughter's life to become a circus, subject to the whims of the Council and regarded as a freak by the whole country." A flicker of unease passed over Elizabeth's face; she did not want it either.

Darcy opened his mouth to deny the fate of vivomancers, but truthfully, he had given it little thought. He had never met the kingdom's two vivomancers. They were not part of the *ton*. However, the Council expected them to be available when they were needed, and they could be summoned at all hours—day or night. He had heard that they lived well, but he wondered if they supposed they could say no to any request. Perhaps there was something to Bennet's words.

Bennet watched him intently. "I hope we can trust you to keep our secret since we are keeping yours."

"Of course," Darcy murmured, still rather stunned. "I do not understand how you manage to conceal such a talent."

"Most of the local people know me only as a healer," Elizabeth said. "They do not know the full extent of my abilities."

Longbourn's isolation from the rest of Hertfordshire was beginning to make more sense. The whole family must labor to hide Elizabeth's magic from the neighborhood. If her talent was widely known, people all over Britain would travel to Hertfordshire to prevail upon Elizabeth for healing of minor ailments, assistance in growing crops, control of wild animals, or any number of other requests.

The world abruptly tilted. Elizabeth rushed toward Darcy and grabbed his arm before he started to fall. Belatedly Bennet seized Darcy's other arm. "Mr. Dee, perhaps you should sit." Elizabeth's words were more a command than a suggestion as she gestured to a nearby bench.

Only then did he realize how much his body was shaking. His legs could barely hold him up. He had expended more energy today than he had in many days, and he was perspiring freely in the warmth of the sun. No wonder he was flagging.

Elizabeth hovered beside him as he trudged to the bench and sat rather heavily on it. Seating herself beside him, she placed her hand on his wrist and closed her eyes, no doubt extending her powers to examine his body. After a moment she announced, "It is only excessive exertion. You should recover your strength after sitting for a few minutes. And I did give you a bit of a boost." She glanced at her sister. "Could you fetch Mr. Dee a glass of water?" Mary nodded and hastened away.

"I will rest my old bones over there." Bennet gestured to a bench around a curve in the path. "Call me should Mr. Dee fall to the ground. I

am not capable of picking him up, but I can summon a few footmen."
With an ironic smile, he ambled away.

Now that Darcy understood how Elizabeth's mancy worked, he
was even more inclined to heed her advice. Vivomancers could literally
peer inside living beings and view how their bodies functioned.

"How did you learn your craft?" he asked her.

"I am mostly self-taught," she responded. "My father purchased
every book available on the subject. Although there are not many, and
some are inaccurate."

Even more impressive. Darcy had benefited from the instruction of
tutors and professors at Cambridge, but Elizabeth had attained proficiency
on her own. Untrained magic could be dangerous; surely vivomancy was
no exception. He wanted to ask more about how her mancy operated, but
Mr. Dee the wool merchant was not likely to have a particularly thorough
understanding of magical theory. Not for the first time he wished he could
reveal the full truth to her.

In this setting, he found her completely enchanting. The sun
highlighted bits of red in her hair and rendered her eyes almost as green as
the grass.

Every time Darcy promised himself that he would quell his interest
in her, she proved to be more fascinating. He realized he was staring at her
and quickly averted his gaze.

It was past time for him to marry and sire an heir. He had a
responsibility to Pemberley. Yet he had never found a woman he longed to
court seriously. If he had found Elizabeth at one of the glittering balls of
London, he would not have hesitated to pursue her. She was everything he
desired: witty, vivacious, and full of magic.

Why did she have to be the daughter of a country squire? Under
other circumstances, he might have permitted himself to fall in love with
such a woman, but recent scandals in Darcy's family demanded that he
marry a woman of good breeding with a spotless reputation. It would be
better to avoid her company altogether. Spending time with her was like
peering in the window of a closed bakery and viewing the delicacies he
could never taste.

There was nothing for it. In a few days he would quit Hertfordshire
and would never lay eyes on Miss Elizabeth Bennet again. He should limit
his time with her to ease the inevitable separation.

He lurched to his feet. "I am quite recovered." She regarded him
dubiously, but he forged ahead. "I should return to the house to rest."

She hurried to her feet. "Of course." She looped her arm through his, a friendly gesture, although they both recognized she was preventing him from stumbling. In this way, they slowly traced their way along the garden pathway toward Longbourn.

***

Ordinarily Elizabeth was not so bold with strange men, but she suspected her patient would be loath to admit he was unsteady on his feet.

Indeed, despite his cane, he stumbled a little on the gravel of the garden path, but Elizabeth was able to prevent him from falling. He grinned ruefully. "My mind supposes I am more recovered than my body is."

"This is a common affliction among male patients," she said acerbically.

"I do not enjoy being an invalid."

He might be in trade, but everything about him suggested a man of great wealth. His speech was refined, and his manners were excellent. His clothing was of the highest quality and perfectly cut. And he had a habit of command, expecting that others would defer to his opinions and obey his orders.

He might not enjoy the privilege of rank, but he clearly possessed greater wealth than the Bennets—the kind of wealth that opened many doors in London. She would not be surprised if he even attended the *ton*'s glittering balls, although she doubted he would take pleasure in them. He was more than a simple wool merchant. But Elizabeth supposed he was entitled to his privacy.

"Nobody does," she observed. "But recovery requires patience. You are recovering from a head contusion, two knife wounds, a fever, a wrenched ankle, and an infection."

After a moment, he said, "I suppose I should be grateful to be alive—let alone that I can walk and talk."

"Truthfully, you are healing quickly. You should not be disappointed with your progress."

"Do you know when I will be completely healed?" he asked.

She shook her head. "Your life energies grow stronger every day, but mancy cannot determine much more with precision."

"How do you sense life energies?"

"I perceive them as colors," she said. "Blue means all is well. Yellow is a sickly color, and red indicates a wound."

"Can you cure anything?"

"Not at all. I do well with wounds and broken bones. But I cannot heal most natural occurrences – cancer, apoplexy, pox—although I can often ease the symptoms.

"How very fortunate for the neighborhood," Mr. Dee said.

She grimaced. "They do not always share that perspective. Many people perceive any kind of mancy as witchcraft. They are suspicious even if they enjoy the benefits."

"It is abominable that the neighborhood treats your family with suspicion because of two mancers in your midst."

"Two? We have seven. We are all mancers."

He gaped. "Seven? How can that be?"

She nodded. "Kitty is a pyromancer, Mary is a terramancer, and Lydia is a ferromancer, although she does not practice much. My mother's magic is mostly with fabric; she created the lovely curtains and embroidered cushions throughout the house. And my father's mancy is powerful with shields and wards."

"*Both* of your parents have magic?" he said incredulously.

"Yes, although my mother is loath to talk about it. I believe she was ridiculed and shunned in her childhood. My father was more insulated by his place in society. Marrying him must have given my mother quite a sense of relief."

"There are many in society who marry their sons and daughters to mages in the hopes that their children will have talent, but there is never a guarantee. Plenty of children never inherit mancy. I have never heard tell of a family in which every child is a mancer. That is quite a blessing!"

He spoke as if he knew a lot about magic, but it was rare in merchant families. Perhaps he had an aristocratic ancestor. "So you do have magic?"

His expression abruptly shuttered. Clearly she had hit upon a subject he meant to keep private. "Yes, I have some small ability," he said in a quelling tone.

"I believe that magic is more of a blessing in London than in Hertfordshire."

"But surely your neighbors benefit from your talents."

"Indeed. They are pleased when we can prevent a fire from spreading, drain a flooded field, or heal a boy's broken arm. They are pleased to bring us presents of game or flowers. But few of our neighbors would wish their daughters to befriend the Bennet sisters, and none desire their sons to court any of us."

"Such a provincial view is unfortunate. I sometimes hear such sentiments in De—the country. In London, though, strong magic is lauded and sought after."

"It has been suggested that we remove to London, but it would be far more difficult to conceal my real talent there."

"Indeed," Mr. Dee agreed. "But you should at least visit town. Your family would find an enthusiastic reception."

"That would be lovely," Elizabeth said wistfully.

"The Council would protect you from those who would want to use your powers unjustly."

"And who would protect me from the Council?" she asked.

He was silent for a long moment. "You are not wrong," he finally said. "Their reputation for ruthless manipulation is not undeserved." They continued in silence for a moment. "However," he said, "there are many other benefits to London society. You and your sisters would be sought after for your magical talents. Many gentlemen would like to make your acquaintance."

Mr. Dee's conduct was puzzling. At times he appeared to be flirting with her, but now he was suggesting she should seek out other men. "Do you wish to help me find a husband?" she inquired with a smile.

He colored. "Th-that was n-not my intention," he stammered. "You have good reason for concealing your true talent, but your sisters need not. They might find gentlemen to their liking."

"That might do very well for Jane—or Kitty and Lydia when they are older," Elizabeth mused. "But we have no acquaintance to introduce them into society."

"Oh, my family might—" He stopped himself. "I may have an acquaintance who might do your family that favor."

Elizabeth suspected he had almost revealed a greater acquaintance with the *ton* than a wool merchant should possess. Part of the mystery that was Mr. Dee. "I am certain my father would be pleased to discuss it with you. Do you participate much in London society?"

He grimaced. "Occasionally. My family requires it." Again, Elizabeth sensed he was concealing something. "But I travel extensively to…conduct business."

"It must be lonely."

This characterization troubled him. "I do not find it so. It is more efficient...less dangerous."

"Dangerous?"

"Less danger from highwaymen and the like," he said hastily. "A single man may travel more quickly and stealthily than two or more."

"I see." They walked in silence for a moment. "Although I take pleasure in a solitary ramble, I am so accustomed to being surrounded by family that I would find it strange to be alone for long. I feel safer with other people around, I suppose. If something goes wrong, there are others to help. We each have different strengths."

He shook his head. "If there is trouble, you must only protect other people."

"Oh my, the life of a wool merchant must be quite a bit more exciting than I imagined."

"There i-is always danger on the roads," he stammered.

They turned a corner and arrived at the door of the house. "Would you prefer to retire to your room?"

"Yes," he agreed. "I will admit to some fatigue."

***

Elizabeth left him at the door, but Darcy did not immediately retire to his chamber. He was busy castigating himself, unable to count the number of secrets he had let slip or almost revealed to her. He had always moved among the elite levels of society without anyone being aware of his work for the Agency, allowing him to note and report on possible magical malfeasance. Never before had he experienced such difficulty concealing his object.

He would prefer to blame his indiscretion on the blow to his head but suspected it had more to do with how he reacted to Elizabeth Bennet's charms. Something about her disarmed his customary reticence and caution. Not only did she cause him to lower his guard, but he also found himself *longing* to confess the truth. Luckily she was not an enemy agent, or Darcy would already be dead.

All the more reason to quit Longbourn as soon as possible. Toward that end he needed to contact Richard, whose silence Darcy found increasingly disturbing. While the Bennet family remained in the garden, Darcy slipped out through the front door. The bright noon sunshine cast sharp shadows across the landscape, which was fortunately devoid of occupants. Even the servants were indoors or tending to the family in the garden.

Standing in the shade of a pine tree, Darcy centered himself, taking deep breaths and burrowing deep into the core of his magic. It was more difficult than it should be, but he managed to draw on his reserves and shape the shadows into the form of an imp. Standing about a foot tall, the shadow imp was vaguely humanoid in shape and appeared to be carved from wisps of smoke.

Shadow imps had no real consciousness; they could only follow a shadowmancer's commands. Darcy handed the imp a hastily scribbled note to Richard. The creature's wispy arms enveloped it, hiding it from view. He then relayed meticulous instructions about where the imp could find his cousin, directing it to conceal itself from all other humans.

He clapped his hands to send the imp on its way and watched as it darted from the shadow of the pine tree to the shadow of the oak beside it—and from there to the shade cast by a series of shrubs. It raced from shadow to shadow until it was lost to Darcy's sight. It would travel in that way until it reached Matlock House in London, moving faster than a horse or a person could travel. It would return to Darcy after delivering its message. Still, the whole process would take several hours.

It was the first magic Darcy had performed since being pulled from the river, and it had depleted his energy. Returning to the house, he trudged up the stairs to his room, where he slept soundly for the rest of the afternoon.

He awoke refreshed and astonished to find that he was eagerly anticipating dinner with the family. He usually found society wearisome. Perhaps he simply craved human company after his long isolation.

Darcy spoke little during the meal but instead took the measure of his hosts. Mrs. Bennet and her younger daughters were often rather crass; his aunts and uncle would have been appalled at their conversation. Elizabeth alternated between blushing at their outcries and stifling a smile.

Mrs. Bennet did at least half the talking. She peppered Darcy with questions about his livelihood and family, forcing him to give evasive answers. She also kept up a steady stream of compliments toward her daughters; Lydia was her favorite, but she occasionally praised Jane or Kitty.

Stupid woman, Darcy thought. *Elizabeth saved my life, and "Mr. Dee" is best acquainted with her. If Mrs. Bennet yearns for a daughter to marry an apparently prosperous wool merchant, Elizabeth is the obvious candidate.* She was easily the most intriguing woman Darcy had ever met. Not only did she wield extraordinary vivomancy powers, but she was beautiful and witty. How could her mother prefer Lydia's vapid giggling or Jane's bland serenity to Elizabeth's obvious charms?

Nonetheless, Mrs. Bennet appeared to have forgotten she had a second daughter. Mr. Bennet favored her in a desultory manner but did not bestir himself to promote marriage for any of his daughters. Their attitude was particularly irritating because Darcy saw no evidence that Elizabeth had any local suitors. He understood about the local prejudice against magic, but even so…were the men in the neighborhood blind? Elizabeth was far lovelier than Jane, whose beauty her mother frequently extolled.

If Darcy were a squire from a neighboring estate, he would have courted Elizabeth from the moment she made her bow in society. He briefly indulged in that fantasy, imagining that his position and hers were relatively equal so he might be free to woo her. It was not the first time that he had wished he were Mr. Dee in truth. It was a wonderful vision, but following that path too far could only end in bitterness.

Once he was healed, Darcy would leave Hertfordshire and probably never encounter the Bennets again. He would have no choice but to abandon Elizabeth to her matrimonial fate, whatever that might be. The thought was surprisingly painful.

Darcy was exceedingly grateful he had concealed his name. Mrs. Bennet would be far too happy to learn about his estate in Derbyshire and ten thousand pounds a year. If she were eager to match a daughter to a well-to-do wool merchant, he could only imagine her frenzy of excitement if she learned Darcy's true worth. The discussion had turned to Lydia and Kitty's recent visit to Meryton and rumors that a garrison of militia might be stationed at the town. Truthfully the younger girls were far more excited at that prospect than the presence of a taciturn guest—which suited Darcy quite well. There had been no further news about mysterious strangers inquiring about men who had been fished from the river. Hopefully the necromancer believed Darcy had drowned.

Darcy's gaze often wandered to Elizabeth. There was something magnetic about the animation in her eyes and the sportive way she spoke with everyone, even the servants. He had even found himself flirting with her this afternoon in the garden. It was so easy to do. She had such lively conversation that he could not help but desire her good opinion. He reminded himself sternly that he could do nothing more than admire her…discreetly…from a distance. It would be unforgiveable to foster any expectations he could not fulfil. *I am staring at her again!* He hastily averted his eyes.

By the end of the meal, Darcy was finding it increasingly difficult to keep his mind on the discussion. He had no interest in the subject at hand and really was only interested in conversing with Elizabeth, but she was too far from his seat to make this feasible. His mind drifted to Richard. Had the shadow imp returned with a reply? Darcy was eager to venture outside and search for the creature.

Finally, Mr. Bennet was ready to end the meal. "Would you care to join us for cards and reading in the parlor before you turn in?" he asked Darcy.

"Er…I would enjoy that," Darcy responded. "But…I thought I might take a walk outside first. I have been confined indoors for so long."

"An excellent idea!" Mrs. Bennet exclaimed. "We should all take a stroll after dinner." Lydia rolled her eyes, apparently no more excited about walking with Darcy than he was.

He silently cursed Mrs. Bennet's matchmaking obsession. Now he would need to find a discreet way to separate from the group and seek the imp.

A few minutes later, Darcy was surrounded by Bennets as he stepped out of the front door and onto the lane running from Meryton to Longbourn. The sun was just beginning to set, but there was still plenty of light. Mrs. Bennet and the younger girls tripped quickly down the lane, chattering about bonnets and ribbons. Jane and Elizabeth joined their father while Darcy deliberately lagged behind, leaning on his cane more than necessary.

Darcy slowed his steps even more, allowing the others to outdistance him as he stared into the shadows. The imp was a creature of shade and secrecy; it would not return to Darcy if he was surrounded by people.

"Mr. Dee?" Elizabeth turned around, regarding him questioningly.

"I am more fatigued than I anticipated," he said. "I pray you continue apace, and I will join you eventually."

He sank onto a bench near a small pond by the side of the lane, hoping the others would forget about him. His hope was in vain. The rest of the party came to a halt and peered at him. Mrs. Bennet pulled Lydia back in Darcy's direction, depositing her on the bench. He sighed. He was more than ten years Lydia's elder.

Lydia sat beside him like a sack of potatoes. Elizabeth lingered nearby, admiring flowers near the edge of the pond. Was she hoping to "protect" Darcy and alleviate his discomfort? He could not help admiring her…particularly when she wore trousers that revealed the shape of her legs.

The other girls accompanied their father for a walk along the lane. Mrs. Bennet had returned to the porch, fanning herself—although it was not particularly warm.

Weary of the strained silence, Darcy said, "It is a pleasant evening."

Lydia nodded. "This is my favorite time of day to watch the sun set."

"Indeed. Much more pleasant than at noon," Darcy replied. He heard Elizabeth snicker; Lydia merely blinked.

"Come along, Lizzy!" Mrs. Bennet called from the doorway to the house. No doubt she saw her second oldest daughter as an obstacle to her matrimonial ambitions. Darcy's irritation flared anew. "I need your help settling in the parlor." With an apologetic shrug to Darcy, Elizabeth hurried to her mother and "helped" her into the house.

Darcy stood, having no desire to be in that close proximity to a girl of such tender years. Leaning lightly on his cane, he wandered about and peered into the shadows, hoping the imp would come to him.

"What are you doing?" Lydia inquired from the bench.

"Admiring the shrubbery," he replied. But then he realized he must distract her attention or she might follow him. "I heard you say something about a new shawl. I am passionately interested in shawls—particularly wool shawls. What variety do you plan to purchase?"

Lydia grinned and took a deep breath. "I desire a shawl similar to one that Maria Lucas has, but in a nicer color. Hers is gray. Not even a pleasant light gray but a really dull dark gray. I was thinking of blue. Not navy blue, which is boring, but more sky blue—which is ever so much prettier, don't you think?" She continued without pausing. "But Mama doesn't think sky blue is practical…."

Darcy tuned out her prattle as he scrutinized the surrounding shadows. The imp was nearly upon him before he noticed it. The creature flew into his hands and made an amusing little bow—its signal that it had delivered the message. There apparently was no return message from Richard.

What did that mean? Darcy pondered that question as the imp disintegrated back into shadows now that its mission was complete. Why no reply? Was it possible the imp had delivered the message to the wrong person? That was supposed to be impossible, but no doubt there was a way to trick the magic. Had the necromancer somehow intercepted his messenger?

He meandered back to the bench. Somehow, unbelievably, Lydia was still talking about shawls. How was it possible to devote so many words to such an inane topic?

But then, miraculously, Elizabeth was by his side. He had not even noticed her emerge from the house. "I doubt Mr. Dee needs quite so much detail about fringe," Elizabeth remarked to her sister.

Lydia was taken aback at the thought. "Would he rather hear about my new bonnet?"

"It has been a fatiguing day for him. Perhaps he would prefer to enjoy the summer night in peace," Elizabeth said.

"Peace—" Lydia started and then stopped. "That is odd. All the crickets fell silent."

Darcy stiffened, realizing she was right.

"The same thing happened the other night," Elizabeth remarked. "And then I heard a rustling sound I thought might have been bats. But the sound was so loud, they would have been huge bats."

Dread crawled up Darcy's spine.

He had supposed he was safe from the necromancer's creatures because he had neither heard nor seen them while he was at Longbourn. But…. "Is your house warded?" he demanded of Elizabeth. Warding, magical shielding, was an expensive procedure that many mancers did not bother to provide unless they had a particular reason to fear magical attack.

"Yes," Elizabeth said. "My father did it himself."

Damnation! Darcy had believed himself safe because he had sensed no dangers since arriving at Longbourn. But it was possible—even likely—that the wards had been protecting him – as long as he remained *inside* the house. Today he had emerged from the house, wearing the amulet the necromancer was seeking.

"There!" Elizabeth cried. "That sound!"

Then Darcy heard it: a rustling akin to dead leaves. A sound he had heard only once before. He whirled toward the women. "Run!" he shouted. "Run to the house!"

Lydia froze in terror, but Elizabeth reacted. Grabbing her sister's arm, she pulled Lydia toward Longbourn. Darcy turned and shouted toward Bennet and his daughters, who were fortunately still within sight. "Retreat! Retreat to the house! Danger approaches!" He saw them halt, spin around, and run back.

It was too late.

Within seconds at least a dozen wights descended from the sky, swirling toward Darcy and the women like a flock of gargantuan bats. Lydia screamed.

Then the wights were upon them.

Chapter Six

Darcy was able to gather shadows around him, obscuring himself sufficiently that the wights could not attack him effectively. But maintaining a screen of shadows taxed his already-depleted energy.

He wrapped shadows around the empty holes that served as the wight's eyes. The creature screamed in frustration, flying randomly as it clawed at its face in an attempt to remove the shadows.

Elizabeth had woven vines and brambles into a sort of shield to protect herself and her sister. With her control of iron, Lydia had produced a long, wicked spear, which she used to slash at the wights from behind the cover of the shield. The wights did not bleed when stabbed, but the spear apparently injured them sufficiently to cause the wounded creatures to fall back.

Darcy was the object of the wights' attack. They were attacking all the humans, but more of the creatures were focused on him than on the others. He was the only one the necromancer could possibly have a quarrel with. "Leave me! Leave me!" he shouted to the others, but either they did not hear or were not inclined to obey.

As the other Bennet sisters neared the scene of the battle, a wave from the nearby pond washed over another wight, swamping it—Jane Bennet's doing. Another wight caught fire, although Darcy could not recall which sister was a pyromancer. A huge pit opened in the ground, swallowing two of the wights. Was it Mary who possessed terramancy? Mr. Bennet followed more slowly, but Darcy guessed he was responsible for the bluish light that glowed around the Bennet girls and repulsed the wights' grasping hands.

Darcy could not help but be impressed with the Bennet family's skills. None of them hesitated to throw themselves into the fray despite facing quite daunting and gruesome opponents. They were all practiced in their craft and worked well together. Nevertheless, the wights were numerous and incredibly strong. Darcy recalled what happened when a wight killed a human victim; he had no desire to witness that happening to a Bennet sister.

"Leave me!" he shouted to the others. "It is me the wights seek!" Elizabeth rolled her eyes, and the others ignored him. Damnation! Why did they have to be so stubborn? Darcy was a stranger to them.

A wight made a lunge for Elizabeth, and Darcy attempted to reach her. But Lydia slashed at the creature and forced it to retreat.

In his momentary distraction, he allowed the shadows concealing himself to thin out. The nearest wight reached out a taloned hand toward Darcy's neck. He dodged away, but one claw scraped across his cheek, drawing blood. He did not even notice the creature's other hand until it was too late. It hooked a talon under the amulet's chain and broke it with a flick of its finger. Darcy grabbed at the amulet, but the wight held it in a bony hand out of reach.

It flew away into the night, no doubt taking its prize to the necromancer.

The attacks did not cease.

Darcy suspected the wight that attacked Tolliver had drained the poor man's life energy—effectively feeding from him. Now that the wights were at Longbourn, they regarded the Bennets as a source of fuel. Darcy cursed himself again for drawing the creatures' attention to the family.

"We must go inside!" Bennet shouted. "The house is warded."

Darcy agreed, but there were too many wights. The house might as well have been on the moon.

Bennet was casting shields over his daughters, but he did not have the power to ward them all at once. And he was failing to shield himself. When a wight landed on his back, the other shields disappeared while Bennet used his mancy to repel the creature.

"Leave me!" Bennet yelled to his daughters. "I will shield you until you reach the house."

None of the Bennet daughters appeared to be listening. Finally, Elizabeth cried, "We will not leave Mr. Dee, and we will not leave you, Papa!"

While Darcy applauded their bravery, he had no desire to be the cause of anyone's death.

He could not deny the truth. Even with their combined powers, the humans were losing the battle. There were simply too many wights, and they were too difficult to kill. Even the ones that had been buried in earth or drowned in water were only momentarily deterred, rising to fight again after a few minutes. Darcy did not know if such creatures could even be destroyed. How did one kill creatures that were already dead?

And the human fighters were weakening. While the wights appeared to never tire, the Bennets could not sustain this fight indefinitely. Despair gripped Darcy's heart.

They would all die.

***

Elizabeth had never felt quite so useless. Kitty used fire to fight the wights while Jane used water. Mary was hurling rocks and burying them in the earth. Lydia conjured iron weapons out of thin air, and her father shielded others with his warding mancy. Elizabeth did not recognize Mr. Dee's mancy, but it was effectively deterring attacks and confusing the wights.

Elizabeth's powers, on the other hand, were of little use.

She initially had endeavored to grab and bind the creatures with vines, but the plants withered instantly upon contact with them. Living plants did not survive contact with creatures of pure death. Elizabeth had then grown a shield of vines around herself and Lydia, but the wights' sharp claws frequently cut through the plants, forcing her to constantly regrow them. She bled from many small cuts.

Unfortunately, vivomancers had limited offensive capabilities. Usually it did not bother her, but her family had never faced a threat like this one.

The wights' very existence disturbed her as well. *They are innocent human spirits forced into this horrific shape and compelled to do the necromancer's bidding. How horrifying to be trapped and used in such a way.* She knew of no way to free the spirits save the death of the necromancer who had summoned them—whoever that might be.

Unsurprisingly Mr. Dee's energy was flagging, and his screen of shadows dimmed. A wight was closing in on him. Everyone was engrossed in their own battles; nobody could go to his aid.

Elizabeth could only imagine how a human would appear after being drained by a wight. The thought was unbearable. Abandoning her screen of vines, she rushed to Mr. Dee's side. She pulled at the wight's arm, but she could not move it as much as an inch.

The wight's mouth had latched onto his neck; life energy was seeping from his body. He was endeavoring to push it away, but his movements grew slower and weaker as his skin took on a grayish pallor.

Elizabeth fought a growing sense of panic; surely there was something she could do.

Since the wight were in want of living energy, perhaps she could provide something else to feed upon. Living energy was the vivomancer's stock in trade. Elizabeth gathered energy from the surrounding shrubs, plants, and grass, pulling the very essence of life itself. She imagined shaping that energy into a ball of white light between her hands.

If the wight was a dead enslaved soul, she would fight it with the power of *life*. Elizabeth pushed the ball of energy toward the wight's back, hoping she might distract it from Mr. Dee. To her astonishment, the energy passed through the creature's diaphanous garments and into the body underneath.

The effect was instantaneous. The wight released Mr. Dee, splaying out its limbs in shock. Elizabeth pumped more life energy into its body. After a moment, the wight went still and expelled a breath—almost a sigh. A sigh of relief?

In the next second, the wight's body disintegrated until nothing remained but wisps of mist. And then those too disappeared. She had freed the spirit.

She stared at her hands in astonishment. How in the world did she possess such power?

But there was no time to marvel. A second wight grabbed for Mr. Dee, who was barely able to stand. Elizabeth blocked it with her body, pushing life energy into this creature as she had before. It dissolved immediately, leaving no trace behind.

Mr. Dee's color was quickly improving. She reached out to steady him, but he shook his head. "Help the others," he said hoarsely.

"I will, but you must go to the house." He appeared about to object. "Please help Lydia to safety," she begged, pointing to where her youngest sister knelt on the lawn, clutching a wound in her side.

Mr. Dee gave a weary nod and stumbled toward Lydia. He helped her stand, and they lurched toward the front door.

Whirling around, Elizabeth grabbed and dissolved a wight that was menacing Kitty. Now that she understood the process, it took less time. "Run for the house!" she urged her sister. Elizabeth moved on to grab a wight that was attacking Jane. By the time she had dispatched that one, the others had recognized the threat she represented and were flying away.

She experienced a pang of regret as she helped her father limp into the house. If only she could have freed more tormented souls. Mary was the last one through the door. She closed and bolted it with an expression of relief.

Longbourn's front hallway resembled a field hospital. Hill and one of the maids were applying dressings to Lydia's wounds. Jane had collapsed, exhausted, on the floor while Mr. Bennet and Mr. Dee shared a bench opposite the door. Their mother stood near the stairs wringing her hands.

"We are doomed! We will be slaughtered in our beds!" her mother shrieked.

"How is that possible?" Elizabeth asked. "We are not in our beds."

There was a brief pause. "We will be slaughtered in the hallway!" her mother cried.

"Father's wards are strong," she reassured her mother. "You are certain the wights cannot enter the house?" she asked him.

He nodded. "They might not withstand a concerted attack from such creatures every night, but we need not worry tonight."

"Oh! My nerves! My nerves!" her mother complained. Mr. Bennet signaled one of the maids to take her upstairs and give her a sleeping draught.

Elizabeth hurried to Mr. Dee. The raw neck wound was bleeding furiously and required most of her remaining energy just to seal it closed. Completely healing it and the scrape on his cheek would have to wait until she rested. His pallor suggested that the attack had set back the progress of his healing.

Her father had a long gash down the length of his leg and a wrenched knee. Elizabeth did what she could. Hill had already dressed the wound in Lydia's side—which was not as grave as it first appeared. Elizabeth began the healing process on Mary's injured ankle, promising to do more the next day. By that point, she was weaving on her feet. Jane gently led her to a chair in the blue sitting room, where the others had gathered.

Hill had laid out tea and lemon biscuits to settle everyone's nerves. After a long silence, Kitty voiced the concern that was on everyone's minds. "Will the wights return?"

Mr. Dee rested his head against the tall back of his chair. "I doubt it. Miss Elizabeth has an effective weapon against them. They can seek easier prey elsewhere."

"Do we know why they attacked here?" her father asked.

Mr. Dee cleared his throat and shifted in his chair. "I imagine they sensed the presence of an amulet I had on my person. The necromancer who summoned the wights desires the amulet. One of the wights tore it from my neck during the battle. Now that the necromancer has it, I believe he has no reason to seek me again."

All eyes were fixed on their guest. "Where did you obtain an amulet desperately desired by a necromancer?" Elizabeth's father inquired with deceptive mildness.

Mr. Dee's expression was stony. "There are things I cannot reveal."

"Magical amulets help sell a lot of wool, do they?" Her father's voice was sharp.

"I will depart from Longbourn if that is your wish, sir," Mr. Dee said calmly. His face was pale, and from the stiff way he held himself, Elizabeth guessed he was in pain.

"You cannot travel," she said flatly. "You would not survive."

"I would not place the inhabitants of Longbourn at risk," he insisted.

"We will be safe if we remain behind the wards," Elizabeth said to her father. "They only manifest at night."

Her father inclined his head. "I am willing to see what happens tomorrow night. However, if the creatures return, we will address the situation again."

"Fair enough." Mr. Dee leaned forward in his chair. "Miss Elizabeth, how did you manage to fight off the wights?"

She glanced down at the hands clasped in her lap. "I cannot say. I had never fought such creatures before, but I was desperate. Since they are things of death, I thought to gather life energy and suffused them with it. I did not know what would happen."

Mr. Dee shook his head. "They are supposed to be indestructible. I believed we were doomed."

"Wights are creatures of death, and you are a mancer who wields the power of life," Jane said softly.

Mr. Dee nodded slowly. "Miss Elizabeth's power may be the sort necessary to defeat the wights." He considered for a moment. "I have reason to believe that the necromancer may send the wights to menace others. Would you be willing to help them?"

"Of course," Elizabeth responded. "You may share my secret with the Agency and Council leadership."

"Elizabeth—" her father said in a warning tone.

She met his gaze. "Papa, I would not stand by and allow others to be killed by such creatures if I might help."

He conceded with a sigh.

"And what variety of mancy did you use?" Kitty asked Mr. Dee. "I have never seen the like."

He weighed his response. Elizabeth had long suspected that much of what he had told the family was a string of half-truths. But her instincts told her she could trust him. He certainly had been eager to protect the others during the wights' attack. But her father was not wrong to worry that the man's secrets might be dangerous to the family.

Mr. Dee sighed. "I am a shadowmancer. I bound the wights' sight with shadows."

Her father raised an eyebrow. "Do you experience many wights attacking your family's sheep?"

Mr. Dee stiffened. "As I am sure you are aware, sir, we are born into our magic, and we are born into our family. Those two accidents of birth do not always coincide neatly."

It was odd. He was a stranger and could be lying, and yet Elizabeth longed to trust him. He exuded such an aura of dignity and honor that she needed to constantly remind herself he was a stranger. She credited him with a genuine concern for Longbourn's safety.

A spot of red was growing on the fold of his disheveled cravat. "Mr. Dee, I believe your wound has opened again." He touched the spot and winced in pain. "You should retire for the night. Let me heal you in your room."

A flash of defiance in his eyes suggested he did not like being ordered about, but he acquiesced with a weary nod, too tired to argue.

They trudged up the stairs in silence. He sank gratefully onto his bed and unwound the neckcloth. The wound was not large, but it had ragged edges, and she suspected such a bite was more difficult to heal than one from an ordinary animal.

"I am exceedingly sorry your family was forced into such a battle," he murmured while she knelt by his side and sent healing energy into the wound.

"Nobody should have to face wights. They are an abomination." I wish I could have fought them off on my own."

She gazed up into his face. "Surely that is impossible!"

"Likely it is. Still, I regret drawing others into the fray."

She tilted her head to the side and regarded him. "Nobody wants to send others into danger, but there is strength in numbers. I might not have discovered my ability to drain wights if my family had not protected me at the beginning of the fighting."

"This is why I prefer to face danger alone. I do not want to be responsible for the safety of others—and they can be unreliable." His face betrayed more than he knew. She wondered who had betrayed Mr. Dee's trust so badly that he hesitated to trust again.

She stood, having finished healing his wound. "I suppose that is one difference between us. If I am facing trials, I would much rather not be alone."

She had opened the door to depart when she heard Mr. Dee's voice behind her mutter, "If you had lived my life, you would prefer it."

***

Darcy slept late the next morning as his body recovered from the previous evening's exertions. The Bennet family had finished breakfast and were in the parlor when he descended the stairs. Having recovered her strength, Elizabeth was able to completely heal the scrape on his cheek and further mend the wound on his neck. Although Darcy was greatly improved, he was still tired and stiff and hoped that he would not need to do more fighting immediately.

He would have expected the wight attack to be the primary topic of discussion, but Mrs. Bennet was effusively reciting news that Hill had gathered during a visit to town earlier in the morning.

"Mrs. Cooper's housekeeper said—" The woman gave a dramatic pause. "Netherfield Park is let at last!" This news elicited squeals of excitement from the younger girls, and even Jane raised her eyes from her embroidery.

Mr. Bennet glanced up from his paper and gestured for his wife to continue relating her story.

"It has been taken by a man of large fortune from the northern part of the country. He is worth five thousand pounds a year!" There were general murmurs of astonishment from around the room.

Darcy fixed his eyes on the opposite wall. Not only was his fortune twice that of this unknown man's, but such an announcement would not have occasioned any exclamations in Darcy's circles. He was experiencing anew the gulf between his world and the Bennets'—a gulf they did not perceive because they did not know Darcy's true identity. How would they treat him if they knew his real name? With awe and deference—as they did this unknown neighbor? In reality, they would probably be furious at his deception. Fortunately, they were unlikely to make that discovery.

At times Darcy had been grateful for his secrecy, but at that moment the deception weighed upon him. The family undoubtedly experienced greater ease around Mr. Dee than they would around Mr. Darcy, but they did not truly know him. *Elizabeth* did not truly know him. What a melancholy thought.

"What is the new gentleman's name?" Kitty asked.

"And when will he give a ball?" Lydia asked.

"Mrs. Cooper and her housekeeper do not know his name, but I assure you I will do my best to discover it so your father might visit him. Mrs. Jameson told her that Netherfield's new owner would be attending the assembly ball with a large party of ladies and gentlemen. That will be a treat indeed! Kitty, you must wear your new gown, and Lydia, we must procure ribbons for yours."

The longer Darcy resided at Longbourn, the more he had sensed the edge of desperation clinging to Mrs. Bennet. She had five daughters with virtually no dowries, and their family was barely tolerated in Meryton society. A wealthy unmarried stranger must appear to be a gift from heaven.

Mrs. Bennet was vulgar, and some of the daughters lacked sense, but Darcy had actually grown somewhat fond of them. None of them lacked bravery; they had protected him from the wights as if he were a part of the family.

Perhaps he might help them once he returned to his life. His Aunt Margaret might sponsor one of the sisters in London society. With their mancy talents, they should be sought after as brides for families with sufficient wealth of their own who wanted to ensure that magic bred true in their lineage.

Kitty and Lydia were too young and flighty for such an honor, and Mary was too sour. But Jane and Elizabeth were quite pretty and very magically talented. But the thought of Elizabeth wedding another man made his stomach churn. *I should be happy if she found a worthy husband,* he admonished himself. *She deserves a secure future,* but he did not want to envision it.

Then he recalled that he could not bring a Bennet daughter forth in society without revealing his true identity. Surely there was some service he could render the family. *Perhaps a gift of some variety? But would Bennet's pride allow him to accept it? Or could I do so anonymously? Damnation! How had the situation grown so complicated?*

"Will you attend the assembly ball?" Lydia asked Darcy.

Darcy had only been giving the conversation half his attention. "I beg your pardon?"

"We will have an assembly ball in Meryton in a week's time. Will you attend?"

Darcy would wager he would be the only attendee who had washed up on the banks of the River Lea. Despite his customary distaste for balls, he found the idea strangely appealing. *I am simply in need of entertainment to break up the monotony. It has nothing to do with the prospect of spending more time with Elizabeth.*

If there were no further wight attacks, attending a ball should be safe enough. It would be a pleasant ending to his sojourn at Longbourn. He might dance with Elizabeth—a memory to carry with him after he quitted the neighborhood forever. "I do not know if I will still be in Hertfordshire...."

Elizabeth gave him a sharp look. "You need at least a week more to recover—unless you wish to court pneumonia or additional injuries."

He nodded, attempting to appear meek and obedient. "I would prefer to remain. I have not fared well by ignoring your medical advice."

She laughed.

The discourse had turned to who would attend the ball when Hill opened the parlor door. "There is a man at the door who said he is seeking his cousin."

Richard! Finally. Darcy climbed to his feet.

He could hear his cousin's voice speaking to a servant in the hallway. Darcy made haste toward the front hall as fast as his battered body would allow. Richard was dusty and travel-stained, but lines of worry around his eyes smoothed out when he saw Darcy.

"Will!" His cousin took Darcy's extended hand and pulled him into a hug, holding him with a surprising ferocity.

"Good Lord, man," Richard whispered into Darcy's ear. "I truly believed we had lost you."

Darcy returned his cousin's embrace. "I apologize. I did send a letter. Did it go astray?"

Richard grimaced. "It must have. I received nothing." He released his death grip on Darcy, who gestured for his cousin to follow him to the drawing room. Darcy would have preferred a private tête-à-tête with Richard, but it would be unforgivably rude not to introduce him to the Bennet family.

"These good people have been taking care of me," Darcy said, identifying each by name.

He introduced his cousin only as "Richard Williams."

Mrs. Bennet took one look at the cut of Richard's suit and decided that he was someone her daughters should become acquainted with.

"Are you also in the wool trade?" she asked him.

Richard looked a little startled. "Not at present. I am in the army."

Lydia squealed. "Did you bring your regimentals? I love a man in red!"

Richard's lips twitched. "No. I do not intend to stay the night." Lydia made a moue of disappointment.

Tea arrived, and the next hour of Richard's life was consumed with responding to intrusive questions from Kitty, Lydia, and Mrs. Bennet, many of which he had to answer as evasively as Darcy had. Elizabeth said little but watched with an appraising eye, no doubt noticing all the things Richard did *not* say.

Eventually the conversation devolved—as it so often did at Longbourn—into a monologue from Mrs. Bennet. She nattered on obliviously about the varieties of wool she preferred and the best colors of dye. Richard listened in bemusement, nodding occasionally. Lydia interjected with questions about his uniform, regiment, and horse.

Darcy was finally free to maneuver Richard outside to the back garden. He was forced to rely on a cane for support as he limped the short distance to the chairs under the oak tree.

Richard's easy amiability with the Bennets had been replaced by a sober look of concern. "I pray you, cousin, tell me what happened. If I had not tasted those lemon biscuits myself, I would have sworn the Bennets were starving you. And you appear to have not slept for a week."

Darcy had a mirror. He knew he was gaunt and pale. "In short: I hit my head, was stabbed by the necromancer's men, and then I fell into the Lea." He gave his cousin an abbreviated account of his travails.

Richard gasped. "One of our agents reported a rumor you had drowned. At first, I did not credit it, but when I receive no word from you, I worried it was true."

"It was a near thing," Darcy admitted. "Elizabeth and Jane Bennet pulled me from the river, and Elizabeth healed me."

"She is the dark-haired one you were staring at?"

Darcy's head jerked up. "I was not staring at her!"

Richard chuckled. "I have never seen you so entranced by a woman. I was beginning to believe you were impervious to their charms." He held up a hand to forestall another protest. "Oh, I doubt any of the Bennets noticed your infatuation. They do not know you as well as I."

Darcy shook his head. "You had better not share these wild speculations with another soul. You know we must both marry women of impeccable breeding."

Richard rubbed his face. "Indeed. I had another lecture from my father on the subject just the other day."

Darcy found himself scowling at his cousin. Being Mr. Dee was so much pleasanter than the man with the weight of so many family duties.

"But Miss Elizabeth's father is a gentleman," Richard pointed out.

Darcy shook his head. "Her mother's family is in trade. Your father and Aunt Catherine would be appalled. It is just as well. She has no desire to be thrust into the public eye." *With good reason.* "And marriage to me would inevitably bring that."

"She does not appear overly shy," Richard said with a frown.

"It is not shyness," Darcy said. "It is…I must tell you something in the strictest confidence."

"Of course."

"Yesterday evening the Bennet family and I were attacked by about a dozen wights—no doubt sent by the necromancer. The creatures retrieved the amulet I had taken before."

Richard gasped. "How did you survive?"

"Things would have gone ill for us indeed were it not for Elizabeth. She was able to destroy the wights because she is a vivomancer."

"A vivomancer!" His cousin took a moment to absorb the news. "Why does the Council not know of it?"

"Her family has concealed her powers for her entire life."

Richard folded his arms over his chest. "And yet you are telling me."

"She has consented for me to share the information with the director and the Council leadership. Cranston should know that vivomancers can destroy wights. He should recruit Britain's other vivomancers in secret, so they are prepared if the wights attack elsewhere."

Richard nodded slowly. "Yes, that would be an extremely valuable weapon. Wights are thought to be indestructible. But two vivomancers may not be sufficient. Will Miss Elizabeth help the Council if they request it?"

Darcy frowned, not liking the idea of putting her in danger. "I believe so. Her family is intent on keeping her talent private, but she has a strong sense of right and wrong. She has saved my life twice."

Richard's eyebrows shot up. "Then I owe her a great debt." Darcy considered how much bigger was the debt *he* owed her.

Darcy glanced at the angle of the sun. "You should depart soon. Until the danger of the wights is past, you should avoid traveling at night." He handed his cousin a scrap of paper. "I wrote a list of the necromancer's followers whom I recognized."

His cousin read the list, eyes widening. "There are prominent names on this list."

"Yes. The movement to use dark magic is clearly more widespread than we credited. And many of the followers were masked. There could be even more prominent mancers among their number. I am only praying there are none on the Council."

Richard winced. "God forbid." He folded the paper and put it in his pocket. "I will take this to the director. This situation is far more serious than we feared."

"Do you think he will have the followers arrested?"

Richard sighed. "He would hate to agitate some of the old families, particularly without more evidence than your word. However, this necromancer threatens everything. I did not know one person could even summon more than a single wight. Such news is quite disturbing."

"There are many members of the Council who will argue against arrests," Darcy said.

"I hope that will not sway the director's decision."

"Which way will your father fall?" The Earl of Matlock was one of the longest-serving Council members.

Richard grimaced. "I do not know. He always says the Council made the right decision about Edward, but I do not know if he actually believes it. For a time, I thought Papa would surrender his Council seat after…but perhaps he did not because he still believes in its mission."

"I hope so."

"I wish you could deliver the report in person, Will."

"I will come as soon as I can. However, yesterday's attack set back my recovery."

Richard clapped a hand on Darcy's shoulder. "Is this family taking good care of you?"

"Yes. I am very fortunate."

"Indeed." Richard grinned. "For that alone I am willing to undergo any number of sighs about regimentals."

Darcy laughed.

They chatted for a few more minutes as Darcy escorted his cousin to the stable. They clasped hands before Richard mounted his gelding and trotted down the drive. Darcy watched until the other man was out of sight, hating the necessity of giving the charge into another's hands.

When Darcy turned toward the house, he found Elizabeth standing in the drive, watching him. "Your cousin has departed already?"

"Yes, I thought it best if he did not travel at night."

"Indeed." She lifted an eyebrow. "And he is taking your important information to the Council?"

Darcy should never underestimate her intelligence. "Why do you say that?"

She rolled her eyes. "You were eager for your information to go *somewhere*. I did not believe it was to the wool merchants' guild."

Darcy laughed. "My cousin has some contacts in the Council. They need to know about the wights as soon as possible." At least that was true—just not the whole truth.

Chapter Seven

On the evening of Richard's departure, Darcy knocked on the door to Mr. Bennet's study.

"Come in."

Darcy found the master of Longbourn seated behind his desk, perusing a book of accounts. He glanced up when Darcy entered. "Mr. Dee. Are you in search of some fresh reading material?"

"No." Darcy closed the door behind him. "I wished to speak with you."

"This sounds serious." Bennet closed his book and gestured to the chair opposite the desk. "Please have a seat."

Darcy sat and cleared his throat. "I am aware that my presence has caused your household considerable difficulty."

"You do not eat that much," Bennet said with a smile.

"I was referring to the attack yesterday and the lengths to which your family has gone to conceal my presence. Not to mention that you will have provided clothing, food, and protection for nearly a fortnight if I remain as long as planned. And I would be dead if not for your daughter's care for my health. I am profoundly grateful."

Bennet waved this away. "It was our pleasure."

Darcy took a pouch from his pocket. It contained a not insignificant number of the banknotes Richard had brought him. He dropped the pouch on Bennet's desk. "I would like to repay your generosity."

Bennet's eyebrows shot upward. "That is unnecessary. You are our guest."

"A completely uninvited guest who nearly caused the death of many members of your family last night."

"I do not hold you responsible."

"And yet it happened. I owe your family an enormous debt. This is only a token recompense." He gestured to the pouch.

"We do not regard you as being in our debt."

"Nevertheless, I would prefer to discharge any obligations so that I need not depend upon—"

"That is the problem, is it not?" Bennet said with a small smile. "You do not like to be indebted to or rely upon anyone else. You would prefer to be independent."

Darcy shrugged. "Would not everyone?"

Bennet frowned. "I do not believe most people would say it was their goal."

Darcy was not sure he believed the other man. Most people accepted dependence because they had no choice. He was thankful that his income allowed him independence most of his life.

Bennet stood, an obvious sign the interview was over. "You have offered, and I have refused. Consider any obligation to have been discharged and think no more upon it."

Darcy had little choice but to accept Bennet's proposal. But he left the room unsatisfied. He must discover some other way to repay the family's generosity.

***

As Mr. Dee had predicted, the wights did not trouble Longbourn again. Perhaps the family's resistance had been too fierce, or perhaps the necromancer was satisfied now that he had possession of the amulet.

Mr. Dee's cousin had given him a sum of money, and the Bennets' visitor put the funds to use the very next day. Since he was no longer concealing his presence, Mr. Dee summoned Meryton's tailor and ordered several suits of clothes made, for day and evening wear. He had been making do with Mr. Bennet's old clothes, a situation that obviously frustrated him—as the garments were both too loose and too short.

Although Elizabeth had not been privy to the man's discussions with the tailor, she later heard a footman telling a maid, "He demanded the very best fabrics Meryton had to offer, and even that did not satisfy him." Elizabeth was a little amazed that a tradesman would be so fussy, but she supposed that a wool merchant would have strong opinions about fabrics.

Visits from other merchants followed, and soon Mr. Dee was outfitted with hats, boots, cravats, and other necessary accessories of the finest quality. With each visitor, her mother's estimates of Mr. Dee's wealth increased. His family's business must be highly prosperous indeed.

Elizabeth encouraged him to gradually increase his level of activity, and he steadily grew stronger. He embarked on a series of walks in the company of various Bennet sisters. Mr. Dee did not wish to be known as the man who washed up on the banks of the river. Therefore, when they encountered acquaintances on their walks, the Bennets introduced him as the son of their father's friend from London. But he was not eager to visit Meryton.

Mr. Dee had been rather proud and formal when he had first arrived at Longbourn, but recently he had acted more relaxed. Perhaps he was simply relieved of an anxiety about bringing danger to Longbourn now that the wights were gone and he had passed his mysterious information on to his cousin.

In fact, this Mr. Dee was quite good company. He and Elizabeth had animated discussions about Byron, various Shakespeare plays, and even *The Mysteries of Udolpho*. He was astonished to learn that Jane and Elizabeth regularly read the London papers and was quite interested in their opinions of recent events. He was curious about the Bennet family's magical training and asked many questions. He knew a surprising amount of magical theory, although she could sense him carefully parceling out his information, leery of revealing too much. She would guess he had been educated at Oxford or Cambridge, which was certainly not common for tradesmen's sons—all part of the mystery that was Mr. Dee.

She knew that Jane and her father had noticed the various inconsistencies and gaps in his story, but by common agreement, they did not press him. Elizabeth guessed he worked for the Council for Enchantment in an unofficial capacity; a wool merchant, who must travel constantly, might be a good agent for them to recruit.

There came a day when none of the other Bennet sisters could accompany Mr. Dee and Elizabeth on their daily walk. He seemed quite disappointed, assuming that they could not walk out together. Elizabeth assured him that she saw little reason for concern if she walked with him alone but suggested they remain on Longbourn property, where fewer eyes would notice them.

She led him on a walk to the river—a different section of riverfront than the one where she and Jane had first recovered him. Their destination was at the end of the lane, where a dock jutted out into the water.

Mr. Dee's face was unreadable, and Elizabeth wondered if perhaps she should have avoided the river altogether. If she had nearly drowned, she might have had an aversion to large bodies of water. But then he strode onto the dock itself, marching right to the end. Elizabeth could do nothing other than follow him.

After contemplating the water for a long moment, he sat at the end of the dock, dangling his legs over the water. Elizabeth scrambled to sit beside him.

They were silent for a long minute. "What do you recollect from your time in the river?" she asked.

He did not answer immediately. "Confused images mostly. The pain of the knife wounds. Splashing into the river. I hoped to reach the bank, but the current was too strong. I thought I would die there. I remember finding the log and clinging for dear life…and then…." He shook his head. "I did not expect to wake up at all, let alone in a clean, soft bed. That was probably more shocking than anything else. I am eternally indebted to you, your sister, and your whole family."

She shook her head. "You owe us nothing."

"Exposing you to the danger of wights is hardly an effective expression of gratitude."

"It is not traditionally considered such, no. May I suggest instead flowers?"

He gaped at her for a minute and then started laughing. "You never say what I expect you to."

"I do delight in being unpredictable."

"Indeed. Most ladies of my acquaintance are far too predictable in my opinion. They worry about saying anything wrong…I wish my sister might meet you."

This was the first time he had mentioned any siblings, and it naturally aroused her curiosity. "Is she also unpredictable?"

His smile faded. "No. Not at all. She is almost painfully concerned with doing the right thing. However, I think a little of your irreverence might do her good."

"I do not believe anyone has ever before suggested I would be a *good* influence."

His gaze was quite intent. "Then clearly you have been keeping company with the wrong sort of people."

Elizabeth had to look away. It was too much. She cleared her throat. "How old is your sister?"

"Fifteen. About your sister Lydia's age."

She decided to pursue this line of inquiry while he was in a forthcoming mood. "Does she live with your parents?"

"No. They are long gone. Right now she resides at my aunt and uncle's house—my cousin Richard's parents—in the country."

With such a gap in their ages, he must have been almost like a father to his sister. He would have needed to grow up very quickly. Another piece of the puzzle that was Mr. Dee.

"We could invite your sister to Longbourn so she might witness for herself that you are well."

"No." His reply was swift and intense.

Did he believe the Bennets were not genteel enough to meet his family? Were the Bennets too bohemian? Elizabeth was wearing trousers today, as she often did when walking about the estate. Did Mr. Dee find that immodest?

After a moment, he fumbled through an explanation. "Although she would be delighted to meet you, this is a part of my life that she does not participate in."

What did he mean by that? She did not participate in the wool trade? Conversing with women on docks? Mysterious tasks that resulted in wight attacks? Although Elizabeth was gratified to know that there were other people in Mr. Dee's life to whom he was a mystery.

She watched his profile as he meditated on the river. He was sometimes imperious and taciturn; however, Elizabeth could not help being drawn to him. He was an exceedingly handsome man. Wherever he went, women must be eager to make his acquaintance. Even Lydia had noticed his comely appearance, although she had pronounced his conversation boring—which Elizabeth could not understand. She thought he was the most fascinating man she had ever met.

"Have you ever wished you were born into a different family?" he asked her abruptly.

"No. I do not believe another family would suit me so well."

"You do not long for a family that would be more popular in the neighborhood?"

She tilted her head, considering. "I do wish we had more friends, but I would prefer to change the neighborhood rather than my family."

His gaze was still on the river, but the twitch of a muscle in his jaw suggested tension. "You are fortunate indeed. I am tied to the weight of familial obligation in everything I do, and I often wish to be free from those expectations. My family has recently been…plagued by scandals, none of which are my doing. My uncle and aunt believe it is incumbent upon the rest of us to do what we can to ensure the family's social standing."

Elizabeth understood all too well how the conduct of one family member could influence the standing of others. How frequently had she been embarrassed by her mother's lack of discretion or Lydia's forward behavior?

He scowled. "My uncle believes it is of chief importance that I marry a woman of good social standing and wealth."

Elizabeth's breath caught. Was this meant for her? A warning against forming expectations? She did not know how else to interpret it. The Bennets certainly had neither standing nor wealth.

Quickly she averted her gaze to the river. The words hurt more than she expected. Had she already formed some attachment to Mr. Dee? She probed her own feelings and realized it was not impossible to imagine herself falling in love with this man.

She could not allow that. Not only had he made his expectations clear, but there also was much about his life she did not know—things he was concealing. He appeared to view her with some affection, but perhaps she was misinterpreting his gratitude for saving his life. Although he appeared to take pleasure in their walks about Longbourn, at times he expressed eagerness to leave Hertfordshire without any apparent regret.

She would do well to heed his warning and guard her heart. Her continued insistence on walking with him every day was foolish. She did not desire to become one of those lovelorn maidens who fell for a rake from London, believing his sweet words. Not that Mr. Dee had uttered any sweet words.

No. Whether or not Mr. Dee had sought to win her good opinion, Elizabeth would be safer distancing herself from him. The logical side of her mind could only conclude that she should avoid him. It was better for her heart and her reputation.

Yet even as Elizabeth drew these conclusions, she knew she would ignore them. He would only remain in Hertfordshire for a few more days. She would not waste those days avoiding him. His arrival had added variety and color to the routine at Longbourn, and Elizabeth had soaked in his company like water in the desert. She could not bring herself to cut off the supply prematurely. Instead, she would simply have to find a way to repair the damage to her heart once he was gone.

Mr. Dee turned to her and gazed into her eyes. She could not have looked away if her life had depended upon it. "There are times…many times lately…that I have wished I was born into another family. That I was free of these obligations and could bestow my heart where I would."

Elizabeth's reserve melted away. It was not a declaration of love, but it was a balm to her heart. She heard his meaning plainly. If circumstances were different, perhaps they might have had a future. It was a small consolation.

How awful to be constrained by one's family in a choice as intimate as whom one wed! Her own disappointment mingled with her sympathy for him. His fingers brushed the back of her hand, a touch she had longed for without realizing it. Shivers shot down her spine.

She yearned for more, much more, and had to remind herself that he had just said anything between them was impossible. *Go now*, she warned herself. *Go, before you give in to temptation.*

She clambered to her feet. "Perhaps it would be best if we return to the house."

***

On the day of the assembly ball, the Bennet carriage was not sufficient to hold the whole party. Mr. Dee volunteered to wait for the carriage's return; perhaps he was not particularly eager to take the trip in the company of giggling and complaining girls. Elizabeth agreed to wait as well, not realizing until too late that they would be the only ones in the carriage. Fortunately, it was a short ride to the assembly hall.

In the three days since their walk to the river, she had avoided being alone with him, but she had enjoyed his companionship when they were in company with others. Their discourse had been pleasant; however, she had successfully avoided the intimacy that had characterized their conversation at the dock.

For the assembly ball, Elizabeth had worn her best white gown with gold embroidery. Although it was modest, the neckline was lower than what she usually wore. A scattering of jeweled pins sparkled in her hair. Mr. Dee's eyes widened gratifyingly when she stepped into the carriage.

Seated on the bench opposite her, he was quite handsome in a dark blue coat and a waistcoat of blue and forest green. "Your gown is…quite striking," he said as the carriage lurched into motion.

"I thank you. This is my favorite."

"The jewels in your hair match the color of your eyes perfectly."

He had noticed the color of her eyes? Flustered, Elizabeth murmured thanks and averted her gaze out the window. *Do not read too much into his admiration.*

"No doubt the men will be queueing up for an opportunity to dance with you."

She laughed, endeavoring not to sound bitter. "I will be lucky if any man invites me to dance—no matter how pretty my gown is."

He frowned. "How is that possible?"

She shrugged. "Nobody is eager to court the witches of Longbourn."

He muttered something about "provincial attitudes."

"Kitty and Lydia do receive a share of male attention," she said. "They are flirtatious and easy in their manner. The men of the village believe I am more…dangerous."

"That is…undeserved," he growled.

Elizabeth's lips twitched at the vehemence of his defense. "Too true. Kitty is far more deadly. She could set them on fire."

He leaned forward, peering deep into her eyes. "They are as blind to your value as they are to your beauty."

Elizabeth knew she should look away. It was inappropriate to gaze at a man so frankly. Moreover, doing so with *this* man could break her heart. But there was something mesmerizing about the dark blue depths of his eyes. *Lord help me, I do not want to look away.*

"I feel extremely fortunate to have made your acquaintance. I hope you will honor me with the first set of dances." Mr. Dee pressed forward until their knees were touching.

Elizabeth's breath caught, and she had difficulty formulating a response. She reminded herself firmly that she had no hopes of this man, but her treacherous heart beat a little faster.

"Miss Elizabeth?" he prompted.

She should refuse. Accepting would only lead inevitably to heartbreak. *More* heartbreak. She had vowed to keep her distance—for good reasons. But she would never have another opportunity to dance with this man. She might never have another opportunity to dance with a man she liked. "Yes. Of course," she replied. Those words were wholly inadequate. "I would be pleased to dance with you."

Perhaps they had no future, but they could enjoy this one night together. Elizabeth could live the fantasy of attending a ball with a handsome man who found her attractive.

Their faces were very close, mere inches apart. Surely this was exceedingly improper. But Elizabeth had no desire to move. He gave her a slow smile. "It is the least I might do for the angel who saved my life."

Elizabeth's fantasy shattered. Of course he was not flirting! He was merely being gallant to the woman who had saved his life. It was akin to dancing with a sister or cousin out of obligation. She leaned back against the squabs and turned her head toward the window, somehow managing a smile. "I have told you before, sir, that flowers are perfectly sufficient."

He chuckled. "But not nearly so enjoyable." She did not respond, and he continued to stare at her. After a short silence, he inquired, "Have I said something to make you unhappy?"

"Not at all."

"I pray you believe me when I say that I think the men of Hertfordshire should not overlook your beauty and charms.

"It is kind of you to say, sir."

He made a frustrated noise. "It is not kind. It is the truth!" He seized her hand and kissed the back. Then he yanked off her glove, ignoring Elizabeth's gasp, and pressed his lips to her palm. The intimacy of the gesture made her blush, but at the same time it was not unpleasant—not at all. She could only imagine what those lips would feel like touching her cheek, her neck, her lips.

"A man could wait his entire life to find a woman such as you, Elizabeth!" His voice was husky with passion.

Those were not the words of a man who merely felt gratitude. And this man did not make such declarations lightly. She was feverish, delirious. With a mere kiss on her hand, he had managed to cause her body to shimmer with happiness.

She longed to declare her own sentiments and throw herself into his arms, containing her impulses with the thinnest thread of reason. He was practically a stranger. He would soon be leaving. He had told her there could be nothing between them.

But she might never experience these emotions again. Perhaps she could forget her misgivings for one night and just take pleasure in his nearness.

She leaned toward him. "Mr. Dee—" The carriage lurched to a halt, and Elizabeth recollected herself. "We are here!" she said inanely. Did she imagine a disappointed expression on his face? She hastily pulled her glove back on.

"Indeed. Allow me." Mr. Dee quickly ducked out of the carriage and then held out his hand to assist her in descending the step. Even through two pairs of gloves, a spark passed from his hand to hers.

He offered his arm as they walked up the steps into the assembly hall; she might as well have been walking on clouds as he escorted her through the entrance. Never before had she entered any gathering at

Meryton on the arm of a handsome man. *I will savor the moment*, she vowed, *and banish any worries for another day.*

The orchestra was still tuning the instruments, so the dancing had not yet commenced. They quickly located Elizabeth's parents near the ballroom entrance—deep in conversation with Jane, Sir William Lucas, and a tall fair-haired stranger.

"Lizzy!" her mother crowed. "You must meet our new neighbor! Mr. Bingley, this is our second eldest daughter, Miss Elizabeth Bennet. Mr. Bingley is the gentleman who has let Netherfield."

Elizabeth curtsied a greeting, but Mr. Bingley was not looking at her. He was staring over her shoulder at the man beside her. "Darcy? What on earth are you doing here?"

Chapter Eight

Darcy attempted to gather his wits as Bingley pumped his hand eagerly, babbling about how he and his sisters had just arrived in Hertfordshire earlier that week. "How do you come to be here?" his friend asked again with a wide grin. Naturally, Bingley would never suspect anything untoward.

Damnation! It all made sense now. The new neighbor from the north of the country with five thousand a year...Darcy might have made the connection if he had been listening more attentively.

There was a long pause as Darcy considered a plausible response to Bingley's question. "They fished me from the River Lea" would only create more questions.

"Mr. Dee...arcy has been our guest at Longbourn for the past fortnight," Mr. Bennet said when Darcy failed to answer. His tone was warm and amiable, but the look he gave Darcy was poisonous.

"I had not the least idea you were here!" Bingley exclaimed. "I thought you were back at Pemberley!"

"Pemberley?" Elizabeth said faintly.

Oh no....

"Darcy's estate in Derbyshire," Bingley said enthusiastically. "Largest estate in Derbyshire and a fine manor house. The work of many generations. Surely you know about Pemberley?"

"Oh...I did not realize his holdings were so...extensive..." Elizabeth murmured.

"Of course not! Darcy here is all modesty."

"That is not the word I would use," Elizabeth said faintly.

Darcy had spent a fortnight carefully constructing a house of cards, and now Bingley was knocking everything down without even realizing it. Darcy had not allowed himself to believe his delicate edifice of lies could come tumbling down so easily—or so spectacularly. He had been quite wrong.

Darcy had expected he would disappear forever from the Bennets' lives, and they would never be the wiser. But here was Bingley, who had no idea that Darcy worked for the Agency or that he might have any need for discretion.

Now Mr. and Mrs. Bennet, Jane, and Elizabeth regarded him with varying degrees of shock and betrayal on their faces. No, strike that. Mrs. Bennet appeared delighted. Mr. Bennet's face was red with anger. Jane was bewildered. And Elizabeth…he could barely stand to behold the pain so naked on her face.

Darcy desperately longed to take her into a quiet corner and explain the whole situation. But he was absolutely forbidden to reveal that he worked for the Agency, and without that explanation nothing else would be believable. Nor would she be likely to calmly listen to an explanation.

Would Elizabeth guess there was more to the story than just a series of lies? Or would she believe he had concealed his identity for nefarious reasons of his own? Or worse, because he was a town dandy toying with the Bennets?

Mrs. Bennet appeared not to care about the truth, only the money. "What a good joke, Mr. Darcy! Not telling us all of that!"

"How odd," Bingley said. "Darcy is not usually one for jests."

Miss Bingley glided up to them. As usual, Bingley's sister was dressed in the latest fashions and held her head high—the better to display her superiority. *Oh joy. Her presence is all that the scene needs for a proper French farce.* "Mr. Darcy!" she exclaimed, standing far closer than was polite. "How unexpected! Did you come just to surprise us?"

"Uh…no…I was visiting the Bennet family at Longbourn."

Her gaze raked over the Bennets. "I did not know you had any acquaintance in this part of the country."

Darcy did not know how to respond to that. The family had been telling people that Mr. Bennet was an acquaintance of Darcy's father, but that would provoke incredulous questions from people who actually knew Darcy's family. "I did not know you had taken a place in Hertfordshire," he said to Bingley, quickly redirecting the discussion.

"Yes, it was all rather last minute," Bingley said. "I visited the place and liked it immediately, so we settled on an agreement that day."

Bingley's sister gave him a fake smile. "I thought you wrote to Mr. Darcy to invite him to Netherfield."

"I did," Bingley explained. "But I sent the letter to Pemberley. It must still be chasing you about the country."

"Yes." Goodness knew where Darcy's post was now.

"Now that you are here, you simply must come to stay at Netherfield!" Miss Bingley exclaimed. "It is ever so comfortable." She regarded the Bennets with a sneer that suggested what she thought of the probable comforts of their home.

Mrs. Bennet drew herself up. "Mr. Darcy is *our* guest."

Miss Bingley took advantage of her greater height to look down at the other woman. "He is one of my brother's oldest friends, and we have not enjoyed his company in ages."

Darcy was beginning to feel like the rope in a tug of war.

Mrs. Bennet looked to Elizabeth and her husband for assistance, but neither would meet her eye.

Miss Bingley applied directly to Darcy. "Charles is in desperate need of your advice about the drains, and the stable is in a dreadful state. I am certain you will know what to do."

"Yes," Bingley agreed. "I was saying to Louisa just this morning, 'I wish Darcy could be here. He would be just the person to help.' Say you will come!"

Darcy's head spun at the speed with which events were moving. Bennet's scowl suggested he was eager to rid himself of Darcy, and Mrs. Bennet apparently had exhausted her supply of arguments. Elizabeth studiously avoided Darcy's gaze. No doubt the whole family would prefer to see the back of a man who had lied to them for a fortnight. "Very well."

Bingley clapped his hands. "Excellent."

The orchestra was playing the opening bars of the first set of dances. "Ah, but we cannot neglect the dancing," Bingley said. "Miss Bennet has already agreed to be my partner for the first set." He smiled at Jane, and she returned a shy grin.

Somehow Miss Bingley had gained possession of Darcy's arm. "It has been too long since we last saw you!" she drawled, eyeing him expectantly. Yes, she was hinting for an invitation to dance.

"Oh, but—" Darcy glanced at Elizabeth, whose lips were pursed, her expression unreadable.

"Mr. *Darcy*," she said, "you have just been reunited with your friends. By all means you should dance with them." Her words were amiable, and no doubt sounded sincere to others. But Darcy could hear a hard edge.

"Nobody dances like you, Mr. Darcy!" Miss Bingley trilled, consolidating her hold on his arm.

No, he would not renege on his promise. "But—" He turned toward Elizabeth to tell her that, but she was gone. How had she escaped so quickly?

Damnation! He could not run about the ballroom seeking her. It would be unseemly, and the director would not thank him for drawing attention to himself. Darcy reluctantly allowed Miss Bingley to tug him onto the dance floor.

***

Elizabeth watched Miss Bingley dance with Mr. Dee—Mr. Darcy—without allowing bitterness to encroach on her thoughts. She had known that the man she had fished from the river was hiding things. And yet she had fooled herself into thinking he had not actually *lied* to her. She had believed somehow that he really was Mr. Dee the wool merchant despite all the inconsistencies in his stories.

But he had been evasive about so many things—as had his cousin Richard, if that was his real name. She was a fool to believe anything Mr. Darcy had told her, and now she was suffering the consequences.

She would never have guessed he was quite that rich, however. The largest estate in Derbyshire! Well, he was far beyond Elizabeth's touch.

As soon as the dancing commenced, Elizabeth's mother went about ferreting out information. Mrs. Hurst, Mr. Bingley's other sister, confided that Mr. Darcy was worth ten thousand a year. This had sent her mother into a frenzy of excitement, strategizing how she might connive to have him invite Lydia or Jane to dance. Elizabeth had entered the ballroom on Mr. Darcy's arm, but she was accustomed to her mother overlooking her. And today it was definitely for the best. She did not need her mother insisting that their erstwhile guest invite her to dance.

Elizabeth was not more inclined to dance with him after learning of his wealth. She had caught glimpses of reserve and disdain in Mr. Darcy's conduct. Now she understood its source; he must have experienced Longbourn as very provincial.

Surely any glimmers of affection she had glimpsed were products of her imagination or wishful thinking. No doubt any tenderness that he exhibited was the result of gratitude for saving his life.

She had cautioned herself against falling in love with him, and yet she had done so just the same. What a terrible moment to realize it. She had fallen for a man who was so far beyond her reach that she would not have even met him if he had not fallen in the river. She had allowed herself to dream about a future with him despite knowing it was a bad idea.

Tears blurred her vision, and she hastened to the ladies' retiring room, which was fortunately deserted this early in the ball. Bad enough that she experienced these emotions for Mr. Darcy; it was unthinkable that anyone else should witness them. Elizabeth positioned herself on a settee and took a few deep breaths, dabbing her eyes.

Her plan had been to wait until Mr. Darcy was free to dance, but now that struck her as a supremely bad idea. Even if she could survive the dance without tears, she would feel like she was eating the crumbs from Miss Bingley's plate. Any pleasure to be had in dancing would be leavened by humiliation. And then Mr. Darcy and his friends would be witnesses to her lack of partners for the rest of the ball.

It would be preferable to claim a headache and return home. If the Bennet carriage could not take her, she could walk. Her mind decided, Elizabeth rose and made her way to the door. She would leave the ball and never have anything to do with Mr. Dee/Darcy again.

He could not be trusted.

***

Darcy gritted his teeth throughout his two sets with Miss Bingley. She chattered on about mutual acquaintances, the shocking gossip from London, and her great pleasure at his company. She required only the minimum of participation from him, so his thoughts were not much engaged. It was unsupportable to exchange Elizabeth's conversation for *this*. How was fate so cruel as to condemn him to such misery when he had been so close to experiencing such joy?

It was a relief when he made his final bow to Miss Bingley and escaped with the excuse of needing to find the privy. When he returned to the ballroom, he sought out Elizabeth, eager to claim the dances he had promised her. The ball was quite a crush; he maneuvered through the crowds slowly, searching for any sign of Elizabeth. Only once he had circumnavigated the entire room did he realize she was not present.

Where had she gone?

Darcy cast about for any member of the Bennet family. Mrs. Bennet or Jane would be most likely to know Elizabeth's whereabouts and most inclined to treat Darcy civilly. Unfortunately, Mrs. Bennet was deep in a knot of chattering matrons, and Jane was dancing with an officer. Mr. Bennet, however, was unengaged and watching the dancers.

Darcy did not wish to have that discussion, but he needed to locate Elizabeth. Bennet regarded Darcy rather coldly as he approached. "I was seeking Miss Elizabeth," he said without preamble. "I had promised her a dance."

The other man's eyebrows rose. "Apparently she did not believe she had promised one to you. She returned home with a headache."

Darcy's heart fell into his shoes. Not only was he deprived of his long-anticipated chance to dance with her, but now he could not explain himself either. He could hardly hasten after her to Longbourn. Now that his true identity was known, he was the object of no small interest at the ball, and his absence would be noted. Worse, they would have few chances for private discourse after he relocated to Netherfield. Bingley had already sent a footman to collect Darcy's things from Longbourn.

"That is a shame," Darcy said. "I hoped to speak to her."

"I daresay she has no wish to speak to you." Bennet's tone of voice could have frozen water.

Darcy took a deep breath. "Mr. Bennet, please believe that I did not set out to deceive your family. There are good reasons I needed to conceal my identity."

The other man snorted. "No doubt."

"There are things I cannot tell you—"

"Yes, yes. Go explain them to your friend Bingley." He gestured toward the dance floor.

Darcy was tired of the man's skepticism. "You need not believe me, but you should at least believe that the wights were not a product of your imagination. Everything I did was designed to keep your family safe from the wights and other...creatures that sought me. If lies were required to keep innocent people safe, then I would tell them again."

He turned on his heel and left a dumbstruck Mr. Bennet behind him.

***

Elizabeth's family appeared to have taken the alteration in their erstwhile guest's identity in stride. Her mother was apt to view it as an opportunity and was only sorry he showed no particular interest in any of the Bennet daughters. Elizabeth's father grumbled whenever the man's name was mentioned but was not inclined to take any action aside from complaining.

Lydia had always thought the man was boring, and Mary considered him insufficiently pious. Kitty was more interested in meeting Mr. Darcy's cousin again. Jane was inclined to believe that their guest must have had good reasons for the deception and, naturally, held no grudge.

Elizabeth was alone in her anger and sense of abandonment. She poured out her heart to Jane. But her sister was caught up in the first blush of love for Mr. Bingley, and Elizabeth was unwilling to spill too much venom on her happiness.

All in all, Elizabeth eagerly anticipated the day when Mr. Darcy quitted Hertfordshire and she no longer need worry that she might encounter him on the streets of Meryton.

A diversion arrived in the form of her father's cousin, a man they had never met before. Mr. Collins, a clergyman from Kent, would inherit Longbourn upon their father's death. After reading his letters to her father, Elizabeth did not have high hopes of Mr. Collins's intelligence, but she at least expected him to be amusing.

Within minutes of his arrival, Mr. Collins made it clear that his object in visiting was to choose a wife from among his cousin's daughters. Elizabeth's mother quickly took him aside and related that she expected Jane to soon be engaged to Mr. Bingley. Unfortunately, that meant his attention fixed on Elizabeth.

At dinner that evening, Mr. Collins maneuvered himself so that he might sit beside her. However, he had little interest in talking about Elizabeth herself. He dominated the conversation with descriptions of the land and house belonging to his patroness, Lady Catherine de Bourgh.

Elizabeth listened to the details of the lady's mantelpiece, windows, and carpets with a sense of wonder…at Mr. Collins's complete sycophancy to his patroness. Only when he mentioned that she was an accomplished mancer was Elizabeth's interest piqued. "What is her mancy?" she inquired.

"She has telemancy," Mr. Collins answered with no little pride in his voice. "And it is quite powerful. She can move large objects with the power of her mind alone. It is amazing to watch."

"Are you a mancer yourself?" Elizabeth's father asked politely.

"Indeed, I am," Mr. Collins puffed out his chest. "And I have spent much time perfecting my powers, particularly so that they might serve the purposes of my noble patroness."

"And what is your mancy?" her father asked.

"It is extremely unusual. Indeed, I believe it is unique. There is no word for it."

Her father raised an eyebrow. "And what is it, pray tell?"

But Mr. Collins was not finished heaping praise upon his magic. "I have not heard of another soul possessing this awesome power."

"Indeed?" Her father gave Elizabeth an amused look.

"Yes." Their guest paused for effect. "I have the ability to instantly set any words to music." When they did not react, he added, "Extemporaneously."

Silence followed this declaration. Elizabeth did not quite know what to say. It was generally accepted that most mancies were useful to the survival of the mage. Such magics would allow individuals to hunt, fight, flee, or survive dangerous situations. She did not understand how singing would do so, but people did occasionally possess odd magical abilities.

Mary appeared intrigued. "Any variety of music, sir?"

"Yes." He cleared his throat. "Any kind that is suited to singing. I could not, for example, set words to a symphony." He chuckled.

"Upon what occasions do you find this talent useful?" her father asked.

"Lady Catherine finds it most pleasing and often calls upon me to demonstrate it in company. I often arrange little compliments for the ladies and find that singing them gives them additional gravitas."

"I see," her father replied, merriment dancing in his eyes. "I am certain that gravitas is exactly what they acquire."

"And," Mr. Collins continued, "When the spirit moves me, I sing my sermons in church."

Her father's lips twitched. "Do you?"

"Yes." The other man puffed up his chest. "They call me the singing cleric of Kent."

"I am quite sure Kent does not possess another one."

"No indeed." Mr. Collins gave a contented smile.

Elizabeth had managed to wrestle her incipient laughter into submission. "Might you be prevailed upon to give us a sample?"

Lydia gave her a horrified look.

"I do not desire to squander this gift," Mr. Collins said primly. "I reserve its use for special occasions."

Such as entertaining Lady Catherine's guests. "I quite understand," Elizabeth said.

"But *you* may be fortunate enough to hear a sample at some point," he said enigmatically.

To Elizabeth's ear, that sounded more like a threat than a promise.

***

When Mr. Collins was not unintentionally amusing, he was tendentious. Partially to escape his stifling presence and partially to take her mind from Mr. Darcy, Elizabeth suggested a walk into Meryton the next day. Unfortunately, their cousin was all too eager to join them. Still, she took pleasure in the fresh air and set such a brisk pace that Mr. Collins found it easier to dawdle with Mary, boring her with tales of his patroness's largesse.

Walking in silence beside Jane, Elizabeth's thoughts inadvertently turned to Mr. Darcy. At breakfast, her mother had relayed the information that apparently Miss Bingley had a secret understanding with Mr. Darcy. Miss Bingley had implied as much to Mrs. Long when accounting for her possessive behavior at the assembly ball. Mrs. Bennet was quite put out that Mr. Darcy had not informed her of this secret engagement.

This information only fueled Elizabeth's anger at the man. He had no business flirting with her if another woman had a claim on him! For a brief shining moment, she had glimpsed a future in which she would not grow old on her father's estate. But it had all been an illusion—fueled by Mr. Darcy's lies.

When they reached Meryton, Lydia and Kitty immediately spied Mr. Denny, one of the militia officers they had met at the ball, and insisted on crossing the street to converse with him. He was accompanied by a new gentleman who had recently joined the militia. Mr. Wickham was particularly handsome, with twinkling brown eyes and an open, cheerful countenance. Elizabeth liked him immediately. Soon she was laughing at his witticisms, completely distracted from her anger at Mr. Darcy.

Unfortunately, it lasted only until Mr. Darcy and Mr. Bingley rode into Meryton. Mr. Bingley immediately struck up a conversation with Jane while Elizabeth's younger sisters continued to chat with Mr. Denny. Elizabeth exchanged a nod with Mr. Darcy but did not speak with him. Mr. Wickham gave Mr. Darcy a smile and nod as if they were acquainted; however, Mr. Darcy glared at the other man and then averted his gaze. How odd! Mr. Wickham huffed a little laugh, shrugged, and turned to join his friend's discourse with the younger girls. He appeared neither amazed nor disconcerted by this rude behavior.

Here was a mystery that Elizabeth was eager to solve. Perhaps Mr. Wickham could shed some light on Mr. Darcy's mysterious behavior. Unfortunately, the militia officers soon departed, and Elizabeth had no opportunity to ask the questions that haunted her.

***

After a week at Netherfield, Darcy was almost completely himself again. His body no longer ached, his energy had returned, and he no longer resembled a wraith in the mirror. He had not recovered all the weight he had lost, but he was much improved.

In many ways the sojourn at Netherfield had everything that he needed: excellent food, comfortable accommodations, endless options for amusing himself, and the company of friends of his station. And yet Darcy was displeased. He even found himself musing wistfully about Longbourn. The Hursts' conversation was insipid, and Miss Bingley's fawning attention grated on his nerves. Bingley was the only company he could stand, and he yearned for more meaningful occupation.

Letters from Richard told Darcy that London had experienced isolated wight attacks. The necromancer was sending the wights to feed from mages' life energies. Following Darcy's advice, the Council had recruited the country's two vivomancers, who had proven effective at destroying the wights, but they could not be everywhere at once.

Darcy had volunteered to return to London to help fight the wights, but the director had ordered him to remain in Hertfordshire to protect Elizabeth—since he was one of the few people who knew the Council could avail itself of a third vivomancer if necessary. When Darcy had read those instructions, he had laughed. How could he protect her when she would not let him near her?

Bingley was enchanted by Miss Jane Bennet and contrived to visit Longbourn frequently. Darcy was more than happy to accompany him. However, Elizabeth was mysteriously absent whenever he arrived. She was indisposed or had gone for a walk or was engaged in practicing delicate spellcraft. Darcy, who longed to explain himself to her, was quite frustrated.

As a result, he was eagerly anticipating the upcoming ball at Lucas Lodge. He knew the Bennets had been invited and hoped he could persuade Elizabeth to dance with him—perhaps even agree to a private discussion.

When they first arrived, he was optimistic. Sir William Lucas actually recommended Elizabeth to Darcy as a dancing partner as she happened to pass by. Darcy eagerly took the opportunity to invite her to dance.

But she declined coldly and continued on her way. Sir William was rather taken aback and soon abandoned the conversation. Darcy asked no one else to dance, ignoring Miss Bingley's increasingly imploring—and then frustrated—looks. He drank wine punch and tracked Elizabeth's movements around the room.

She danced with a man in clerical garb who had trouble recalling the steps. A careful inquiry to Lady Lucas revealed that the man was Mr. Bennet's cousin, who was a guest at Longbourn. Elizabeth did not appear eager to continue the discourse with the man after their set was finished, and he was soon dancing with Miss Charlotte Lucas.

For the next hour she chatted with friends, but nobody approached her to dance. That pleased the jealous part of Darcy's soul but made his heart ache on her behalf. Could no other man perceive how wonderful she was?

However, the ballroom was full of militia officers who did not know the Bennet family's reputation or share the provincial prejudice against magic. Darcy knew it was only a matter of time until one of the officers invited her to dance. But when it happened, it was as if Darcy had been plunged into an icy bath.

Wickham was leading Elizabeth onto the dance floor.

Chapter Nine

I had an opportunity to dance; I did not take it, Elizabeth reminded herself as she watched the dancers in front of her. But the reminder that she had declined a dance with Mr. Darcy did little to assuage her usual sense of isolation at gatherings such as this.

Perhaps it was because she usually had her sisters for company, but at today's event, Jane danced with Mr. Bingley, and her other sisters were accompanied by militia officers. She exchanged pleasantries with some of the local women, but as usual, they kept her at arm's length.

It hardly signifies. I do not need their friendship, and I am not in a dancing mood. Being near Mr. Darcy only stirred up longing and loss—a bitter reminder that she had not made much progress at falling out of love with him.

"Miss Elizabeth?"

Elizabeth started. Lost in thought, she had not noticed Mr. Wickham. "I beg your pardon!" she stammered. "I was woolgathering."

"A woman as lovely as yourself need never beg anyone's pardon," he said smoothly. Elizabeth knew it was empty flattery but was still grateful he made her feel attractive. He sketched a little bow. "I sought you out in the hopes that you might be amenable to partnering me in the coming dance."

Why not? The man was charming and graceful. She had no doubt he would be a good partner. "I would be delighted."

"I am honored." He held out his hand, and she took it.

She was correct that Mr. Wickham was an elegant dancer. It was a joy to stand up with such a handsome and adept partner. Her curiosity regarding his relationship with Mr. Darcy was rewarded early in the set. "Are you well acquainted with Mr. Darcy?" he asked.

"Not well, no," Elizabeth responded. *Particularly since I only just learned his real name.*

Mr. Wickham frowned rather theatrically. "But I heard that he accompanied your family to the assembly ball."

"He did. But he had only been visiting for a few days. He has a distant connection to my family. When he encountered his friend Mr. Bingley, he immediately removed to Netherfield, and we have seen little of him since then." This explanation would account for any bitterness Mr. Wickham heard in Elizabeth's voice.

"That is not particularly friendly of him, but I am not astonished," Mr. Wickham said sourly. "Did anything about him strike you as unusual?"

Elizabeth was immediately wary; she knew that Mr. Darcy had secrets to hide. "Not particularly. Why do you ask?"

"He is an accomplished shadowmancer. I thought he might have demonstrated some tricks."

"Indeed?" Elizabeth raised an eyebrow. "Shadowmancy is so rare. I would be interested in a demonstration."

"You witnessed nothing unusual around him?"

The man is indeed fishing for information. Does he somehow know about the wight attack?

"He *is* unusually proud," she replied.

Wickham chuckled. "He is indeed." Then the man sobered. "You must be careful of Darcy," he warned. "He is not all that he pretends."

"Indeed? He is pleasant enough, although his words are few."

"I know him better than most," Mr. Wickham exclaimed. "My father was the late Mr. Darcy's steward."

"Really?" Elizabeth was astonished.

"You were surprised at the cold manner of our greeting."

"I must confess that I was," Elizabeth replied.

"Darcy and I were raised practically as brothers. His father made a provision for me in his will: a living that was to be mine. But when it fell vacant, Darcy refused to give it to me."

"That is terrible!" Elizabeth was horrified by the story, and at the same time it did not sound like the Mr. Darcy she knew. He had not been petty. He had lied, but not for personal gain, she was certain about that. Something greater was at stake.

Mr. Wickham practically preened at Elizabeth's horrified reaction. "His father was a great man. He would deplore what his son has become."

Elizabeth widened her eyes, acting the gullible country maiden he expected. "What has he become?"

The officer shook his head sadly. "Darcy has grown more and more eccentric. He increasingly eschews society and travels around England on secretive missions pursuing mysterious objects." He lowered his voice. "Some even say he is practicing dark magic."

"Merciful heavens!"

Mr. Wickham continued in this vein, fully confident that Elizabeth would believe every word he said about Mr. Darcy. Elizabeth did not dispute with him; indeed she could not, since she did not know the facts of the events he described. But she believed them to be highly unlikely, and she wondered at the officer's motives for spreading such disparaging information.

How easy it would have been to believe Mr. Wickham's story. It was well-crafted and told with just the right hints of diffidence and bitterness. How plausible it sounded! Mr. Wickham was quite eager to charm her and spoke of yearning to encounter her again. She would have been flattered if she did not suspect he had other motives for his apparent attraction to her.

Believing her wide-eyed credulity, Mr. Wickham soon inquired about how Mr. Darcy had come to Longbourn and what he had been doing since his arrival. He was surprisingly confident that she would provide intimate details about Mr. Darcy that she would not ordinarily share with a stranger.

She told him little, implying that she found Mr. Darcy boring and had spent little time with him. While this appeared to gratify Mr. Wickham's vanity, he grew more and more frustrated that she did not provide him with the information he was seeking.

I must warn the rest of my family to guard their tongues around Mr. Wickham, Elizabeth thought as the dance came to a close. Although she could not know the man's motivation, he appeared intent on damaging Mr. Darcy's reputation.

When the dance ended, Mr. Wickham was all gallantry and brought cups of punch to her and Jane. He repeated the same story about Mr. Darcy to Jane, but her response shocked Elizabeth. She gasped. "Thank goodness he no longer resides at Longbourn. We must do our best to avoid him in the future."

Elizabeth was unsure how to respond. Jane was always determined to think the best of everyone. It was most unlike her to immediately condemn someone, particularly Mr. Darcy, who she had defended to Elizabeth just the day before. "If…you wish," Elizabeth finally said.

She quickly scanned the ballroom for Mr. Darcy; it would be mortifying if he should come upon them discussing his character. But she saw him slipping out of the French doors to the terrace. That eased her mind a little.

As they continued to talk, Jane instantly believed everything Mr. Wickham said without hesitation. How odd! When Mr. Denny, Lydia, and Kitty joined the conversation, Mr. Wickham repeated the story to them, and they also believed it without reservation. Elizabeth said little, but she did intervene to prevent her sisters from revealing much about Mr. Darcy's stay at Longbourn.

Mr. Wickham did little additional dancing. As he circulated among the guests at the ball, she saw him relate the story to their neighbors. Mr. Darcy's name was being blackened before her eyes. She was observing a process akin to the spreading of a plague—jumping from person to person.

Elizabeth reached out with her magic to sense any mancy at work. It was so subtle that she noticed nothing at first, but Mr. Wickham exuded a peculiar variety of magical energy that was directed at whoever he was speaking with at the time.

The magic took a shape unlike anything Elizabeth had perceived before, a very subtle and insinuating mancy. It must be pensimancy, the ability to influence other people's thoughts. It was a rare magic and supposedly regulated by the Council, although she doubted the Council even knew of Mr. Wickham's existence.

If Mr. Wickham was using his magic to turn people against Mr. Darcy, then he was extremely dangerous. Did he simply detest his former friend? Or was he in league with the necromancer who stalked Mr. Darcy? She wished she knew more about the man's shadowy opponent.

As she watched person after person fall under Wickham's spell, Elizabeth realized she was the only one who had resisted. What made her special? She thought it unlikely that vivomancy provided any special protection. Perhaps she was simply best acquainted with Mr. Darcy's character, but Jane's acquaintance with the man had provided no protection at all. Of course, Jane was not in love with Mr. Darcy.

Oh.

Perhaps that is the difference.

Unfortunately, it was not a protection Elizabeth could easily bestow upon others.

As she was pondering that question, Mr. Wickham requested another dance with her. Elizabeth was beginning to loathe Mr. Wickham but considered she might gain more information about the man's motives and methods. And he was an able dancer who suggested she was desirable when nobody else had asked her to dance. So she smiled and said yes.

***

Darcy should not watch. The sight made his stomach churn sickeningly, and yet he could not tear his eyes away. He had escaped to the terrace to avoid the sight of Elizabeth and her sisters enjoying an animated discussion with Wickham, but he needed to know what was happening. The unknown was by far the greater horror, allowing his imagination to prey upon him.

But he had returned to the ballroom to find Elizabeth dancing with Wickham a second time—after refusing to even consider dancing with Darcy. She was touching Wickham's hand, laughing at his witticisms, smiling, and tossing her head flirtatiously. She would probably let him kiss her. And Wickham was in his element; nothing made him happier than charming a vulnerable young woman. Although Elizabeth was far less empty-headed than his usual fare. No doubt he had guessed Darcy's interest in her and decided she was worth pursuing.

Darcy's insides burned as if he had swallowed hot coals. He seethed. And there was nothing he could do. He should quit the ballroom, but some stubborn, foolish part of Darcy believed that he could protect her from Wickham if he remained within sight. It was a ridiculous conceit. Wickham's danger to Elizabeth was in the poison he was undoubtedly pouring into her ear.

At least she had reassured him that she and her family would keep his secrets. He believed she would be on guard even against someone as practiced and smooth as Wickham. It hardly mattered what Wickham knew. He was a blackguard, but he had no magic and was not a disaffected younger son of an aristocrat. He would have nothing to interest the necromancer. His greatest danger was to Darcy's reputation, and nobody in the *ton* would pay heed to his words.

It was rather cold comfort.

At the moment, nothing could be further from Darcy's mind than the Agency's mission. The sight of Elizabeth was too entrancing—even when she was holding Wickham's hand. Why did she torment him so? He knew he could not propose to her. Why could he not simply let go of her?

The realization opened like a hollow pit in his stomach.

I am in love with her.

Fortunately, the surrounding noise muffled the sound of his accompanying groan. He had never been in love before. No wonder he had not recognized the sensation. He briefly put his head in his hands. He instinctively knew that he would not recover from this infatuation quickly. Elizabeth's dark curls, laughter, blue-green eyes, and vibrant conversation would continue to haunt him long after he returned to London.

But the realization altered nothing. Darcy could not marry her. They could not even be distant acquaintances.

It would be best if he left her vicinity. Perhaps the infatuation would fade with time and distance. Yes, that was the solution. He was finally well enough to travel by horseback. He would borrow a horse from Bingley and ride to London. Truthfully, he could have done so at any point that week, but he had dallied because he had longed to speak with Elizabeth. The director could send a stranger to watch over her; it would be equally effective.

He wanted to account for himself and alter her thinking, but that was his pride talking. What did it signify if she loathed him? He would never lay eyes on her again. He had attempted to explain his conduct to her, but she had assiduously avoided him. It was not his fault if she remained in ignorance. His conscience was clear.

In fact, Darcy saw no need to remain at the ball. The hour was yet early for a retreat, but he could claim indisposition. He was weary of the whole affair. Other guests were even viewing him furtively and whispering behind their fans. Women who had been tossing him flirtatious looks were now avoiding his gaze. He was all too familiar with the ways that gossip spread in society. Had Wickham started some new rumor about him?

Darcy did not possess the energy to fight it. He did not possess the energy to care what Hertfordshire society thought about him. He only cared about Elizabeth's opinion, and she was dancing with Wickham. Why should Darcy remain?

Yes. Darcy would return to London as soon as he could extricate himself from Netherfield and have a substitute sent from the Agency. Throwing himself into his work would distract him from a pair of too bewitching green eyes. His mind decided, Darcy returned his gaze to Elizabeth, drinking his fill of her face when she was happy: her smile, her laugh, her beautiful dark curls.

He would not return to Hertfordshire. It did not matter that he felt as if his insides were being scraped out by a knife. He would survive. Somehow.

***

The day after the ball at Lucas Lodge, Mr. Darcy accompanied Mr. Bingley yet again on a visit to Longbourn. Having no desire to speak with the man, Elizabeth took herself outside for an "urgent" gardening chore.

Unfortunately, greater dangers awaited her. Mr. Collins had laid an ambush.

"My dear cousin!" he said, hastening toward her. "I am so pleased you are here. I thought I would need to send a maid to summon you. It is as if we have one mind!"

Elizabeth found this image so disturbing that she did not reply.

Mr. Collins took her elbow and led her to a patch of grass in the shade of a maple tree. He stood a little away from her and posed as if he were about to give a speech or sing an aria....*Oh no*....

"Almost as soon as I entered the house, I singled you out as the companion of my future life." But Mr. Collins did not just speak these words; he sang to the tune of a doleful ballad. "My reasons for marrying are, first, that I think it a right thing for every clergyman to set the example of matrimony in his parish. Secondly, that I am convinced it will add very greatly to my happiness."

Mr. Collins had lowered himself to one knee. Unfortunately, it had recently rained. Within seconds, mud coated his whole left leg. "Thirdly – which perhaps I ought to have mentioned earlier – that it is the particular recommendation of Lady Catherine de Bourgh. Twice has she condescended to give me her opinion: 'You must marry. Choose a gentlewoman for my sake, and for your own; let her be an active, useful sort of person, not brought up high but able to make a small income go a good way. This is my advice. Find such a woman as soon as you can, bring her to Hunsford, and I will visit her.'"

At the pace of a ballad, all of this information passed by sluggishly. And it must be said that Mr. Collins did not possess the best singing voice. The man's voice was thin and reedy and only occasionally in tune. Elizabeth would have expected a passable voice for singing to be part of his mancy, but apparently his "gift" consisted entirely of the ability to set words to music—which was extraordinary as the words of his speech did not easily fit the pattern of a ballad.

Elizabeth yearned to interrupt the man since she had no intention of accepting his proposal, but she could not bring herself to be so rude to someone who was offering marriage. Nevertheless, her ears were growing numb from the onslaught of sound.

Now he was singing about how he would never complain about her small dowry. "On that head, I shall be uniformly silent. You may assure yourself that no ungenerous reproach shall ever pass my lips when we are married."

Elizabeth could not allow this to pass without interruption. "You forget that I have made no answer. I am very sensible of the honor of your proposal, but it is impossible for me to accept it." Naturally, she *spoke* her words, as if she were the straight man in a musical hall farce.

To her surprise, Mr. Collins's tune switched to a sprightlier folk song. "Young ladies usually reject the addresses of the man whom they secretly mean to accept. I am by no means discouraged and shall hope to lead you to the altar ere long." He was still kneeling but had unwisely switched legs, so now his right leg was also coated in mud.

Elizabeth rolled her eyes. "I am perfectly serious in my refusal. You could not make me happy, and I am the last woman in the world who would make you so."

Mr. Collins's music had turned more martial and strident—as well as louder. "When I speak to you next on the subject, I shall hope to receive a more favorable answer." He lunged forward, perhaps with the intention of taking her hand, but he stumbled and fell against her skirt, coating it in mud. "I beg your pardon."

Elizabeth's sole aim at this point was to finish the conversation and escape the man's irritating presence. She quickly stepped away from him and replied, "I know not how to express my refusal in such a way as may convince you of its being one."

"You must give me leave to flatter myself that your refusal of my addresses are merely words—"

He was interrupted by the sounds of someone crashing through the bushes. A male voice calling, "Miss Elizabeth!"

Mr. Darcy? Oh no! It could not possibly be—

The man himself burst into the clearing, shadows at the ready to fight off attackers. His gaze went from Elizabeth with a skirt coated in mud to Mr. Collins kneeling in the mud itself. If only the earth would swallow her up right now!

Mr. Darcy was the last person she desired to witness such mortification. Mr. Collins attempted to scramble to his feet, slipped in the mud, and fell on his face.

Mr. Darcy pulled himself up short. "Er...Miss Elizabeth...I stepped outside Longbourn House and heard the most appalling noises. I thought you were under attack. Are you well?"

"Yes, quite well, thank you." Elizabeth knew her face was turning red.

Mr. Collins had managed to leverage himself from the mud and into a standing position. "The singing was merely part of my proposal."

Mr. Darcy blinked several times. "That was singing...?" His eyes grew wide. "Proposal?" Elizabeth closed her eyes, wishing she could teleport herself to a remote island.

"My mancy is the ability to set words to music."

Mr. Darcy squinted at him. "Are you certain?"

"Y-Yes? I was just using my talent to propose to Miss Elizabeth."

She suspected Mr. Darcy was aware that the ability to produce cacophony was not a quality she sought in a future spouse. He rubbed his chin. "What, precisely, were you proposing to do? Destroy her hearing?"

Mr. Collins drew himself up. "It was—is—a proposal of marriage."

Elizabeth was grateful that Mr. Darcy appeared more appalled at the other man's presumption than amused. His amusement might destroy her.

Mr. Collins regarded Mr. Darcy with impatience, eager for him to depart. But the other man did not take the hint; a corner of his mouth quirked upward. "I understand. Well, carry on." He seated himself on a nearby bench, watching with avid interest.

"This is usually a private activity," the cleric said icily.

Mr. Darcy nodded. "Yes, I understand. But I need to speak with Miss Elizabeth and have not had the opportunity for a week. I cannot let her out of my sight lest I miss my opportunity again."

Elizabeth bit her lip against the danger of laughter. "Actually, sir," she said to her cousin, "since I have already declined your proposal"—was that a smile on Mr. Darcy's face?—"perhaps I might as well speak with Mr. Darcy." Although she had been avoiding him all week, he was the lesser of two evils at the moment.

"But I anticipated pressing my suit a second and even a third time," Mr. Collins said, causing Mr. Darcy's eyes to widen with shock.

"Mr. Collins does not believe my first refusal was serious," she explained to Mr. Darcy.

Mr. Collins nodded, somewhat bemusedly, lowered himself to one knee, opened his mouth, closed it again, and scrambled back to his feet. "Your presence, sir, is rather intrusive," he grouched to Mr. Darcy.

"Perhaps you should give me time to consider your proposal," Elizabeth suggested to him. "It is a momentous decision."

"Ah...hmm...yes," Mr. Collins said. "But don't consider for too long. It is by no means certain that another offer of marriage will ever be made to you."

Scowling, Mr. Darcy surged to his feet and advanced on a startled Mr. Collins. "I do not know why you would say so, sir. In addition to being ungentlemanly and abominably rude, such a statement is patently untrue. Miss Elizabeth is beautiful, witty, accomplished, and a talented mancer. Whoever wins her hand will be a very fortunate man."

Mr. Collins had shrunk away from the onslaught of Mr. Darcy's icy disdain. "Of-Of course."

But Mr. Darcy was not finished. "Perhaps you should do Miss Elizabeth the honor of believing she knows her own mind and was perfectly frank in her refusal the first time."

"Er…yes…I-I s-suppose I shall return to the house." Mr. Collins turned and hurried away.

***

Darcy waited until the cleric was out of earshot. "I hope you are not distressed that I chased off your would-be fiancé?" he inquired of Elizabeth. She had not seemed enamored of the man, but he had belatedly realized that perhaps she had been steeling herself to accept his offer out of a sense of duty to her family—which would be travesty of the highest order.

She appeared to be holding something back. Tears? "No," she said in a strangled voice. And then burst into laughter.

Relieved, Darcy released his laughter as well. Collins had been altogether ridiculous, from his horrid singing to his mud-covered clothing to his entitled assumption that he deserved Elizabeth.

The laughter died down, but then Elizabeth said, "He has the voice of a dyspeptic frog." And more merriment ensued. She wiped tears from her eyes. "Truly, I must thank you for sending the man off," she said to Darcy. "Although I fear he will prevail upon me again."

"You are not planning to accept him?" The thought, no matter how unlikely, filled Darcy with horror.

"Heavens no!" she exclaimed. "My mother would be pleased since he is to inherit Longbourn. But no inheritance is worth a lifetime of that-that singing!"

"I believe caterwauling would be a more apt word."

"I will not dispute the description."

Their laughter spent, silence fell between them.

This was Darcy's chance to say his piece. He cleared his throat. "I must apologize for being…less than truthful with you."

Her face went still. "For lying about your name, your occupation, your place of residence, and nearly every other pertinent fact about your life?"

He stiffened. "It was necessary. When I first awoke at Longbourn, I did not know if I could trust your family."

"And after we healed you, fed you, concealed you, and helped you fight off the wights, you still did not know if you could trust us?"

He frowned. "No, I did come to trust your family. But it was safest for everyone if I maintained my anonymity while there was any chance the necromancer was searching for me. And there are many things I cannot discuss. Not only for my protection but for the protection of those around me."

"So I have surmised. I have narrowed down the possibilities to either a spy for Napoleon or an agent for the Council's Assessor's Agency."

"I am not a French spy!" Darcy said indignantly.

The corner of her mouth curled upward, and he realized what he had tacitly admitted. She was too clever by half. Damnation! He was supposed to be a *secret* agent.

He sighed, acknowledging the truth of her assumption. "I must conduct my affairs in the utmost secrecy. Even Bingley and my sister do not know about…certain parts of my life."

She crossed her arms over her chest. "However, they are fortunate enough to know your real name, occupation, and place of residence. Unless those are lies as well?"

"No."

"You say you trusted us. Then why did you not reveal your real identity? After the wights acquired the amulet, there was no need to hide."

Darcy shrugged. "It was simply easier to continue with the false identity. There is never a good time to reveal a lie. I thought it would not matter in the end."

She stiffened. "You planned to quit Hertfordshire without ever informing us that we had entertained Mr. Darcy, master of Pemberley, for a fortnight."

It sounded despicable when she said it that way. But honesty was the only way through this awkwardness. "That was my scheme, yes."

"Because you did not want anyone knowing that Mr. Darcy had associated with the lowly Bennets of Longbourn." Her mouth was twisted in a harsh line.

"No!" He was appalled she believed that. "No."

"Then why?" she demanded.

"I…suppose I enjoyed the fantasy of being simple Mr. Dee the wool merchant. He could be friends with your family. He had no need to maintain his station. He was free to…admire you." *I did not take the time to savor that experience when I had the chance*, Darcy thought sadly.

"Oh." Elizabeth's eyes went very wide.

"But that is the problem with fantasies, is it not?" His voice sounded bitter. "I am not Mr. Dee. And Mr. Darcy's world came looking for me all too soon."

"Are you promised to another? Do you have an understanding with Miss Bingley?"

"No!" *What a terrible thought. Where had she heard that rumor?* "But I am not free to follow my heart…" he fumbled. "My family has been racked with scandals. My father was arrested for misusing his magic." Her eyebrows climbed in surprise. "We managed to keep it from the papers, but everyone in the Council knows. He died before facing the indignity of a public trial."

"Ah," Elizabeth said. "I wondered who had betrayed you so badly."

He grimaced. "You know me well. But that was not the only time. More recently, there was…a scandal involving my cousin Edward, Richard's brother, and a sordid use of mancy. His other brother John, the viscount, married a woman of dubious reputation. My aunt and uncle have made it clear that they pin their hopes upon me to redeem the family honor. They expect me to marry a woman from a highly regarded family."

Elizabeth bit her lip. "That must be a heavy burden to bear."

"At this moment, the burden is nearly unbearable," he admitted to her. "I cannot tell you how badly I wish I were someone else."

She lifted her chin. "Thank you for telling me the truth."

Darcy had laid his heart on the grass at her feet for her to examine. But it was the right thing to do. "Do you forgive me for my deception?"

"Yes," she said without any hesitation.

He stood a little straighter, a weight lifted from his shoulders. "I must warn you that the necromancer is using wights to attack mages in London. The Council is using vivomancers to fight the scourge, but the director may inquire if you are willing to join the fight."

She regarded him seriously. "I would be willing, but I must discuss it with my father. He has worked so assiduously to ensure the secrecy of my magic. I cannot bring myself to simply discard it."

He nodded. "I will relay that message to the director. I plan to leave for London tomorrow."

She looked everywhere but at him. "I will miss you."

Such simple words. How did they make him ache with longing?

She cleared her throat. "I must tell you that Mr. Wickham has been blackening your name throughout Meryton."

Darcy sighed. "He always does that."

"Did you know that he is a pensimancer?"

Darcy's jaw dropped open. "A—No. Surely you are mistaken!"

"Not at all. I watched as he turned opinions against you throughout the ballroom yesterday. He even convinced *Jane* that you were not to be trusted."

Darcy rubbed his jaw. "I wondered why she was glaring at me in the parlor. But I have known George Wickham my whole life; he has never demonstrated any mancy."

Elizabeth shrugged. "Perhaps he concealed it from you, or perhaps the ability came to him late in life."

"And he did not attempt to persuade you of my perfidy?"

She colored and stared at her shoes. "He did, but apparently I am immune to his…charms."

And here Darcy had been anxious that she preferred Wickham to him! Could he have received any greater proof of her preference?

"Elizabeth…." He could not stand it any longer. He crossed the two feet of space between them in a single step and pulled her into his arms. He expected her to stiffen, but instead she melted, conforming to his body as if they were one person. How could it possibly feel so right to hold her when he knew it was so wrong?

He had only intended an embrace, but it was not enough. Not nearly enough. He tilted his head down as her face rose to meet his. Their lips came together. The kiss was desperate—as if each supplied the air the other needed to breathe. It was a goodbye, but at the same time he did not understand how such a thing was possible. This dance of lips and tongues was the most wonderful sensation he had ever experienced. He never wanted it to cease and was not sure he could survive if it did.

Chapter Ten

This had been a supremely bad idea. Now he would always know what he was sacrificing. He was experiencing a paradise he could never have again.

"Lizzy!" A female voice called from far away.

Their lips separated, and they tore away from each other.

"Lizzy?" He thought the voice might be Kitty's.

"I am coming!" Elizabeth called. She stared at Darcy, her eyes wild with passion and her breathing heavy. He knew the experience had been as revelatory for her as it had been for him.

"I must beg your pardon," Darcy said in a low voice. "I did not intend—"

She rolled her eyes. "Do not apologize for kissing me like *that*. If I had not desired it, I would have prevented you."

Darcy experienced relief and regret mingled together. She would be well within her rights to claim he had compromised her, and he could not deny it. Although he had no desire for scandal, part of him would be overjoyed at being compelled to make her his wife.

"I think it would be best if you quit Longbourn before we are tempted to repeat such…mistakes," she said. With a last regretful look, she turned and hurried toward the house, leaving Darcy to find his way back to Netherfield.

***

The following day, after breakfast, Elizabeth escaped the house for a walk. Just being in the same room with Mr. Collins was awkward. She had finally convinced him that she would not accept his proposal. That evening he used the tune of a popular hymn to propose to Mary. She had declined, saying she was not planning to marry. Elizabeth supposed that Kitty would be next.

She set off in the direction opposite to the road that led to Netherfield; she needed nothing to prompt thoughts of Mr. Darcy. Her thoughts wandered in that direction nonetheless. When would he leave Hertfordshire? Had he already departed? Would he think of her when he was in London? Even if he had no plans to marry Miss Bingley, would he someday marry a woman like her? She wished to divert her thoughts back to the beauty of the trees and nature around her, but they would drift toward Mr. Darcy once again.

The road turned and led her into an area the locals called the Old Forest; it was not a terribly original name, but it accurately described the atmosphere. This area was hilly and stony, so it was densely forested and had never been transformed into farmland. A local viscount owned the land and had once used it for hunting, but the house and grounds had fallen into disuse. The dense foliage did not allow for much sunlight to penetrate. Elizabeth loved the unspoiled, wild woods, but there was no denying they were dark and forbidding.

She took pleasure in the coolness of the sudden shade but could not suppress a slight shiver. There had always been rumors about ghosts and trolls in the Old Forest. Local children would dare each other to venture off the road and into the forest. Elizabeth had always been eager to take a dare, much to Jane's dismay, and had gone further than any of the local boys. Though none of them had truly ventured very far into the woods, always remaining within sight of the road. *I am a grown woman, not subject to childish imaginings*, she reminded herself.

She was a bit relieved to hear the rattle and squeak of a carriage coming up behind her; at least she would briefly have company in this gloomy place. She stepped to the side of the road to allow the carriage to pass. But, to her astonishment, the reins rattled, and the driver commanded the horses to come to a halt. She turned just in time to watch Mr. Wickham jump out.

Elizabeth blinked in surprise. Where in the world had Mr. Wickham obtained a carriage?

She was still wary of the man, but there was no harm in being pleasant. "Mr. Wickham, what brings you here?"

He moved with great agitation, and his voice was high with anxiety. "Your father has sustained a blow to the head! Your family sent me to find you."

"Oh no!" It had not been long since Elizabeth had left Longbourn, but accidents could happen so quickly. She made haste toward the carriage. Her father would need her healing powers immediately. "Has the doctor been summoned?" she asked.

"I do not know."

Mr. Wickham took her hand to help her into the carriage. Elizabeth hesitated. *I vaguely recollect something about this man. Something about his conduct at Lucas Lodge...What was it?*

"Miss Elizabeth?" he inquired.

She had frozen in place. He was untrustworthy in some way, but did it matter when her father was injured?

"We must make haste. Every minute is precious!" he urged.

The answer came flooding back to her. The man was a pensimancer. He could influence people's thoughts with magic and had done so at the Lucas Lodge ball. A quick search with her magical senses determined there was mancy at work. He was influencing her to climb into the carriage.

Fortunately, pensimancy was not strong magic. It could influence the direction of someone's thoughts, but it could not control them, especially if that person was on guard.

When she examined Wickham's story, it became laughably implausible. How would he know her father was injured? He was not a frequent guest at Longbourn. Where had he obtained the carriage?

Mr. Wickham must have some other motivation for wanting her to enter the carriage—which was a compelling argument against it. Even now he was watching her with a convincingly worried expression.

She removed her hand from the man's grasp. "I cannot travel alone with a strange man. I will walk home to Longbourn."

He gaped. "But, surely, under the circumstances—!"

She shook her head, backing away from the man. "No, my father would be the first one to disapprove." *It is a good thing Mr. Wickham does not know Papa.*

The man reached out his hand, increasingly desperate. "Miss Elizabeth, I implore you! Your father's life could be at stake." She could sense the force of his magic, pushing against her resolve.

"No. I will return to Longbourn on my own."

Wickham sighed. "You leave me little choice, madam." Without warning, he leaped forward and grabbed her by the wrist, dragging her toward the carriage. "Conners!" he called to the coachman. "Come and help!"

Elizabeth struggled to free her wrist, but Wickham was much stronger. She shrieked and dug in her heels—all the things that he would expect her to do. But she was also surveying the surrounding greenery for possible weapons. Ah, ivy, that would do very well. It was an aggressive plant that loved to climb all over everything.

She focused her will on the patch of ivy by the side of the road and pushed life into it. She could sense the plant awaken and start to grow, excited at its newfound vitality. She directed it toward Wickham while simultaneously wedging her heels behind a tree root to halt her forward momentum.

Wickham brushed off the first ivy that crept across his boot, but the vine was nothing if not persistent. It worked its way up both of his boots, entangling his feet. He stared down with such an expression of dumbfounded shock that Elizabeth almost laughed. "What devilry is this?" he cried as it rapidly twined itself up his legs.

Pulling out a belt knife, Wickham slashed at the ivy, which was now encircling his waist. He managed to cut one vine, but the plant was growing new shoots far more quickly than he could sever them.

The coachman had climbed down from his perch but was obviously reluctant to go near Elizabeth. "It's the forest!" he exclaimed. "At the inn, they said the Old Forest is haunted!"

"It's not haunted, you fool!" Wickham bellowed. "Come here and help me!"

Elizabeth sent tendrils of ivy creeping toward the coachman, whose eyes grew as wide as saucers. The man frantically sought an escape, but they were surrounded by woods on all sides. After a moment's indecision, he jumped to the carriage, wrenched the door open, and climbed in. A second later, the door lock clicked. Elizabeth chuckled. At least he would not give her any more trouble.

"I know you're doing this, you witch!" Wickham flourished his knife at her even as the vines entangled his arms. "Release me!"

Elizabeth backed away, intending to run toward Meryton for help. But her magic would fade once she quitted the area. When the ivy released him, Wickham would be free to follow her in the carriage. She had to flee where the carriage could not go.

Without another thought, Elizabeth spun around and dashed into the densest part of the Old Forest.

***

Darcy had informed Bingley of his imminent departure, merely saying that business called him back to London. Bingley had been quite startled, and Miss Bingley had pouted. Nonetheless, Darcy planned to leave in the early afternoon.

The encounter with Elizabeth in Longbourn's garden had left Darcy even more torn about his departure. If he had no intention of marrying Elizabeth, he should quit Hertfordshire and remove himself from the temptation of her presence. But the thought of leaving her behind was painful, and he would need to make arrangements with the director to ensure her safety. No matter what he did, she would continue to haunt his thoughts. He had watched Bingley court Jane Bennet with joyous ease, envious that he could not experience such freedom.

Bingley's valet was performing the actual packing, but Floyd regularly consulted with Darcy about his preferences for which items to take and how to pack them. With each decision, Darcy's heart grew heavier. How could he possibly be thinking of sacrificing Elizabeth? She was the best thing that had ever happened to him. He would never find another woman who suited him so well.

When this fantasy grew too appealing, he imagined the scene if he presented Elizabeth as his intended bride to his aunt and uncle Matlock. They would be shocked. They would sneer. They would give Elizabeth the cut direct. They would ensure that he and Elizabeth became persona non grata in the *ton*, rendering it impossible for Darcy to be an agent. What sort of life would that be for Elizabeth? She had grown up in social exile; surely she hoped that marriage would better her circumstances. No. Quitting Hertfordshire was the only answer.

Darcy had arrived at Netherfield's drawing room to bid adieu and give thanks to his hosts when Richard arrived. The door opened, and the butler announced, "Colonel Fitzwilliam," just before the man himself strode in.

Bingley shook Richard's hand heartily. "What a wonderful surprise!"

Darcy watched as Richard bowed to the ladies and Hurst. His cousin's grim expression told him this was not a spontaneous social visit.

"So what brings you to this part of the country?" Bingley asked.

"Urgent family business, I am afraid," Richard said. "Might I speak to Darcy in private?"

"Of course," Bingley said at once. "Darcy, why do you not take the yellow parlor?"

Darcy's heart was pounding by the time he and Richard had settled into chairs in the parlor. Although it was possible his cousin had actually arrived on family business, it was far more likely that an Agency crisis had erupted. And Darcy could imagine far too many disasters. "What is it?"

Richard's countenance had lost all the amiability he had exhibited for Bingley's family. "Grim news from London, I fear. Baldwin and Lady Genevieve are both dead."

The Oxford professor and the dowager countess were the only two known vivomancers in Britain. Darcy gasped. "What happened?"

His cousin shook his head sadly. "Assassinated in their homes."

"Surely they were under guard."

"They were. Baldwin's killer managed to slip into the house and stab him without the guards noticing. We do not know how Lady Genevieve perished; there was not a mark upon her body. We might have chalked it up to natural causes if it had not occurred the same night as Baldwin's death."

"This is terrible!"

"It is a disaster. Council mages have encountered the wights four times in London. Thanks to your advice, we were prepared with the two vivomancers at hand. They wielded the only magic that can destroy the wights. Other mancers can stop them only temporarily."

Darcy leaned back in his chair. "Thank the Lord nobody knows about Elizabeth except you and the director."

Richard's expression remained apprehensive.

Ice gripped Darcy's heart. "That is still the case, is it not? I gave strict instructions."

"*I* told nobody beside the director, but there may be a leak in the department. Information that should have been secret has been compromised recently. Miss Elizabeth's identity may be known to the necromancer."

"Good God!" Panic compressed Darcy's chest. "He could be stalking Elizabeth even now!"

"We have every reason to believe he is in London."

"You had every reason to believe he could not assassinate Baldwin and Lady Genevieve," Darcy snarled. "I am unwilling to gamble her life on that assumption." Richard recoiled at his cousin's vehemence.

Darcy surged to his feet. "He could arrive in Hertfordshire as easily as you could! Or he might have sent some of his followers."

"The director sent me to prevail upon Miss Elizabeth to visit London. We need her to help fight the wights."

Darcy scowled. "No! It is far too dangerous."

Richard's eyebrows shot upward. "I realize you have feelings for Miss Elizabeth, but surely it is her decision."

Darcy stalked to the door waving his hand dismissively. "We are getting ahead of ourselves in any event. First, we must ensure she is safe."

"Immediately?" said Richard.

But Darcy was already in the hallway. "We must go to Longbourn and warn her. There is no time to lose!"

Richard did not share his cousin's sense of urgency, but he gamely followed along.

It took longer than Darcy would have liked for the groom to saddle two horses, but soon they were galloping on the road toward Longbourn. Darcy's anxiety allowed him to outstrip his cousin, and he was the first to rein in his horse at the Bennets' front door.

He slipped out of the saddle and strode up to the door, but it opened before he knocked. Jane Bennet, beleaguered and hollow-eyed, emerged. Wailing emanated from inside the house.

"Mr. Darcy," Jane said, "I hope you can help us. Lizzy is missing!"

Chapter Eleven

Bennet brought Darcy into Longbourn's drawing room—where he described the particulars of the situation. Elizabeth had ventured out for a walk, as was her wont, but she had not returned in a timely manner. Thinking she might have been injured, Bennet had sent servants seeking her along her usual paths, but they had found no evidence of her.

Darcy could hardly contain his anxiety. It was possible she had encountered a mishap such as an injured ankle. But it was far more likely the Necromancer was responsible for her disappearance and he could not help recalling what the man had done to England's other two vivomancers. Perhaps she had merely been abducted. And what had his life come to when that was the best he could hope for?

Mrs. Bennet invited Darcy to sit, but he could not bear the thought of confining himself to one place. Instead, he ranged around the drawing room, endeavoring to satisfy his need for immediate action.

When he had last viewed her, framed by the blossoms in the garden, she had been so winsome. He had thought her the most beautiful creature he had ever beheld, and yet he had only spoken of the constraints on his life and how he must leave Hertfordshire. How could he have been so cruel? Why had he not at least related how important she was to him? It was such a miracle to have captured even a small measure of her regard.

He had been prepared for the idea that he might never encounter her again. But the idea that she might not continue to live in the world was insupportable.

Richard had joined them and was having a terse discourse with Bennet about where they had searched when Colonel Forster arrived. He related the disturbing news that Wickham was missing as well, and a fellow officer had glimpsed the man on a back road riding in a well-appointed carriage. Darcy barely managed to stifle an oath.

The colonel looked pained as he delicately inquired of Bennet, "Sir…is it possible that your daughter accompanied Mr. Wickham…er…willingly?"

Richard's eyes went wide, and Darcy's stomach sank. Elizabeth had danced two sets with Wickham at the Lucas Lodge ball. She had smiled and obviously enjoyed his company. An elopement was the obvious conclusion that the entire neighborhood would draw. And Darcy could not say that they would be wrong. Was it possible Wickham had turned the full force of his pensimancy on Elizabeth and convinced her to run away with him?

Darcy's legs buckled, and he fell into the nearest chair. His gut churned sickeningly. It was quite horribly possible. He could be smooth, charming—everything Darcy was not. She had known Darcy would not marry her. Had Wickham used his magic to present himself as a cure for her heartbreak? Oh, Elizabeth...she would be lost to Darcy forever.

"No." Jane stood up. "Lizzy would never do such a thing! She never confided in me any particular affection for Mr. Wickham, and even if she possessed it, she would never want to bring scandal upon our family."

Bennet nodded. "Well said, Jane. I agree."

Pensimancy could not be used to force a person to do something against their nature. An enormous weight had been removed from Darcy's chest. He could breathe again.

Richard spoke up. "And there is the matter of the carriage. Someone lent it to Wickham. He did not have the funds to buy or rent such an equipage. That suggests he has a patron who wished him to...locate Miss Elizabeth for some other object." He exchanged a look with Darcy; they both knew the necromancer was well-born and was likely to have such a carriage.

Colonel Forster raised his eyebrows. "A patron who wanted Wickham to abduct a young woman?" His eyes were wide with horror. "Toward what end?"

Richard stepped forward. "It is time I revealed myself. I am Colonel Richard Fitzwilliam, a representative of the Council's Assessor's Agency." Forster nodded while Bennet looked shocked. "I believe Miss Elizabeth's abduction is related to an investigation our Agency is conducting into a necromancer." He was careful not to glance at Darcy. While Richard was an acknowledged agent, Darcy's role was secret.

"A necromancer?" Jane said. "The one who sent the wights?"

Bennet jumped to his feet and pointed an accusing finger at Darcy. "This is all your fault, is it not? My daughter has been caught up in your web of lies!"

Darcy said nothing and forced himself to meet the man's accusing gaze. He was bound by multiple oaths not to reveal anything, but he knew in his heart that Bennet was right. None of this would have happened if Darcy had not been foolish enough to entrust Elizabeth's secret to the Council.

Richard interposed himself between Darcy and Bennet, speaking in a low, soothing tone. "Darcy became *inadvertently* involved in a case I am pursuing—"

Bennet snorted disdainfully. "Inadvertently? Pah!"

"—involving an unknown necromancer who is undoubtedly of noble lineage."

"An aristocratic necromancer? Good God!" Colonel Forster gasped.

"The man may be mistaken about the Bennet family's involvement in my case or how much they know. He may have enlisted Wickham in an attempt to glean information from Miss Elizabeth." It was a rather thin explanation for recent events, but it satisfied the colonel. "Now we must search for the carriage." Richard addressed Forster. "Can your men help?"

"Of course!" the colonel replied immediately. "I am ashamed that one of my officers is involved in such a sordid business. I will go to the garrison this minute and arrange for all available men to search the surrounding area."

The minute the colonel had retreated from the room, Bennet strode toward Darcy. "They were right! I trusted you, but there is something dark in your soul—"

"Sir!" Richard interrupted. "I must ask you, who is the source of these aspersions cast on Darcy's character?"

Bennet looked confused and turned to his wife. "Where did you hear it, Mrs. Bennet?"

"It was all from Mr. Wickham!" she said shrilly. "He explained everything at the ball."

Richard crossed his arms over his chest. "This is the same Wickham who we suspect of attempting to kidnap your daughter. Perhaps we might disregard his opinion?"

Bennet rubbed his hands over his face. "Yes, yes. That would be best. What a muddle." He stared at nothing for a long moment. "I will send out my servants again. They know the area; perhaps they can locate this carriage." He strode from the room.

Darcy shook his head. "A swift carriage could be halfway to London by now."

"Perhaps…with a cooperative abductee," Richard said. "I only met Miss Elizabeth once, but I cannot imagine that she would be easy to abduct."

Darcy's lips twitched. "True enough." He stood. "I will send a note to Bingley. He and his staff will undoubtedly desire to help search."

But before he reached the door, it swung open, and Colonel Forster burst into the room, waving a piece of paper. "Just now I received a note from my clerk. Two of my officers found a coachman in Meryton by the name of Conners, who swore that the vines attacked him in the Old Forest. He was hired by Wickham, and Conners can take us to the place."

***

Elizabeth's breath came in ragged gasps, and the brambles caught at the hem of her skirts, but she dared not slow her pace. As she crashed through the undergrowth, she could occasionally discern the noises of pursuit. She could not discern if it was one man or two following her, but she was in danger either way. Wickham would have no trouble finding the trail of broken twigs and flattened grass she had left behind.

Coaxing the ivy into doing her bidding had consumed most of her magical reserves; she was not equal to repeating the trick. Flight was her only hope.

She climbed hills, dodged around boulders, and ducked under branches. She endeavored to hold her skirts up, but too often she needed her hands to navigate the terrain. Despite the sunlight, the forest floor was dark, and she often stumbled over tree roots. *If I had enough time, I would climb a tree.* Even in a dress, she had practice in tree climbing. Unladylike pursuits offered some advantages.

But she could always hear Wickham following her, never far enough away that she could take the time to hide. And she was slowing down. She attempted to dig deep and find a little more energy, but her legs were like lead weights. The air she dragged into her lungs burned like fire.

She stumbled. *No, no! Keep going!* her inner voice screamed at her. She regained her footing and pushed through, climbing a steep hill. And then Wickham was in front of her.

She slammed to a stop, momentarily astonished. He grinned. "You didn't notice the short cut, did you?" He gestured to a quasi-path that led to the top of the hill.

She started to back away, but it was too late. Wickham grabbed both her arms and threw her to the ground. Her head cracked on a rock, creating stars in her vision and causing darkness to encroach around the edges. She struggled to remain aware as the world spun and lurched around her.

Wickham's face loomed above hers. He smiled grimly. "You should have just climbed into the carriage. It will be troublesome walking you back to the road." He pulled out a knife and held the point to her throat. "I would just as soon slit your throat, but my master wants you alive for some reason."

Elizabeth endeavored to muster coherent thoughts through the pain and dizziness in her head. She reached out to the plants and animals around her—birds, rabbits, ivy, trees—but she could touch nothing outside her own body. Fatigue and the head injury combined to limit the reach of her mancy.

Wickham held a second knife to her right hand. "However, he never said you must be delivered with all of your fingers intact...." The knife was very sharp; she could feel the edge cut into the skin above her index finger.

Now she had to fight her own sense of rising panic. She could touch her own life force, which she only used for healing—the last thing she wanted to do to Wickham. But healing was similar to what she had done with the wights—pushing life energies into them—and that had caused them to dissipate. What would happen if she did that to Wickham? He was obviously not dead, but it was worth the attempt.

She gathered her life energies, imagining it as a bright white ball—a tiny sun—and pushed it into the man, just as she had with the wights. At first nothing happened. Wickham still held the knife to her throat. Then he blinked and stopped, frozen in mid-action. He fell backward, crashing limply onto the forest floor. Both knives dropped from nerveless fingers.

Did I kill him? The thought pricked her conscience. Although he had been about to cut off her finger, she did not long to kill him.

Any attempts to sit up made her dizzy and nauseous, but she was able to extend her senses enough to discern a faint pulse and the rhythm of Wickham's shallow breathing. Thank God! She was a healer, not a killer.

Darkness encroached around the edges of her vision; she could not escape its pull any longer. Fighting her attacker had used the last of her energy. She could only pray that Wickham did not awaken before she did. That was her last thought before she fell into the blackness.

***

"Elizabeth? Elizabeth!" Someone was calling her name from very far away. "Elizabeth? Darling?" Who would address her in such a way? Jane? But it was a man's voice.

She managed to crack open her eyes despite their absurd weight. Mr. Darcy was staring down at her, his face creased with worry.

She mumbled something; although it failed to emerge as coherent words, he appeared reassured. "Thank the Lord! What did Wickham do to you? Where are you injured?"

She spoke slowly and carefully with a tongue that was quite uncooperative. "Hit my…head on…rock." Indeed, the pain from the back of her head was a dull throb alternating with occasional piercing stabs.

"She may have a contusion of the brain," said a male voice on her other side. She rolled her head to the left and saw Colonel Fitzwilliam. Why was he in Hertfordshire? Behind Mr. Darcy, she saw a few militia officers. How had so many people come to be in the Old Forest?

Mr. Darcy's fingers felt the back of her head. She winced when he pressed on a particularly tender spot. "My apologies," he said hastily, removing his hand. "There is a lump but no blood," he told his cousin. "Does it hurt anywhere else? Did you break any limbs?" He spoke loudly despite crouching directly beside her.

She wet parched lips. "No, nothing else hurts very much. My hearing is intact as well."

Colonel Fitzwilliam chuckled. "As are her wits."

Mr. Darcy glanced at the colonel. "We must take her back to the carriage. The doctor can examine her at Longbourn."

"Mr. Wickham?" Elizabeth asked hoarsely.

The colonel smiled grimly. "He is here."

"Alive?"

He frowned in confusion. "Yes, but unconscious without a mark upon him. Would you like to explain how you managed that?"

Elizabeth shook her head and then regretted it. "Later." The story was too complicated. "Do not allow him…to escape. He…attempted to abduct me."

Mr. Darcy made a noise like a stifled oath. The colonel's expression was forbidding. "We feared as much."

"He will not escape," Mr. Darcy reassured her. "Richard wrapped his wrists in some sturdy ropes. We have a couple of Colonel Forster's militia officers with us; they can carry him to the road, where he will be taken to the brig."

"We will need to question him first," the colonel cautioned. "He is the only person who knows the necromancer's identity."

Mr. Darcy scowled. "Indeed. I will leave that task to you and the director. I might be tempted to break something." He turned his attention to Elizabeth. "I must pick you up now," he said gently. "I fear it may hurt."

"I understand," she whispered.

He put one arm under her legs and the other around her back, lifting her as if she weighed nothing. It did jostle her injured head, and she could not stifle a moan.

"Perhaps if you position her head differently—" Colonel Fitzwilliam suggested, stretching out a hand.

Mr. Darcy stepped backward, taking her out of his reach. "Do not touch her," he growled at his cousin, who looked shocked, his hand arrested in mid-motion.

Why was Mr. Darcy behaving so? He never spoke that way to anyone, let alone his cousin, with whom he had always been on good terms.

"She is mine to care for," Mr. Darcy said in a more conciliatory tone. "It is my error that placed her in this position." The colonel nodded but regarded his cousin as if he had turned into a wild animal.

Mr. Darcy tilted Elizabeth's body until her head was resting on his shoulder. "Are you comfortable?" he murmured to her.

"Comfortable enough."

She heard grunts and shuffling that suggested the officers were picking up Mr. Wickham—none too gently.

"Richard, if you could lead the way?" Mr. Darcy asked.

"Yes," the colonel said, with an odd note in his voice. "We need to go in this direction."

Elizabeth rested her head against Mr. Darcy's shoulder, safe and protected for the first time in hours.

***

The walk back to the carriage seemed to take twice as long as the trek out, but Darcy would have been happy to carry Elizabeth three times that distance now that he knew she was alive. She had fallen into a swoon again, which was probably for the best given her obvious discomfort. Even when he laid her carefully in the carriage, the motion did not awaken her. Then he sat beside her and carefully laid her head on his lap to prevent her from being jostled.

The militia officers had swung Wickham none too gently into the back of their wagon and set off for the garrison's brig. The man had not awakened. How had Elizabeth incapacitated him? Darcy wondered what the doctor would find when he examined the blackguard.

Richard sat across from Darcy as the carriage bounced and squeaked its way back to Longbourn. He had said nothing about Darcy's outburst, which had startled and disconcerted Darcy himself. *I should apologize*, he thought for the thousandth time. *But perhaps it was best not to call further attention to the incident.*

Seeing her injured and vulnerable had prompted a visceral, possessive reaction in Darcy. At that moment, he could not suffer anyone else to touch her. He might even have snapped at Jane Bennet. Darcy blew out a long breath, willing himself to relax from the frenzy of anxiety over the past hours. He could not exhibit such conduct in front of her family at Longbourn.

He needed to be honest with himself. While Elizabeth would recover from her injuries, Darcy was not sanguine that his possessive behavior would disappear. It was rooted in his deep love for her, which was not likely to wane. If he was unable to conceive of another man touching her, how could he leave her behind in Hertfordshire, knowing that someday another man would marry her?

The mere thought caused cold shivers to run down his spine.

For days, Darcy had agonized about family, duty, and honor balanced against his love for Elizabeth. But perhaps the decision had been made for him. He was beginning to believe he simply could not live without her in his life. The soul-wrenching terror he had experienced when she was missing was perhaps a sign about what he must do.

He had believed he had a choice about marrying Elizabeth Bennet.

He had been wrong.

Clearly this was the woman he was destined to marry. No other woman would suffice.

He would be proud to have her on his arm. Not only was she beautiful and witty, but she also possessed a rare and amazing power. Somehow she had fought Wickham to a standstill. When they had followed their trail, Darcy had every expectation that they would find Elizabeth's body. His relief that she breathed was so great that he had barely restrained himself from kissing her—in front of Richard and Forster's officers.

Of course, it did not excuse his behavior toward Richard. Even if she had been his acknowledged fiancée, it did not justify practically laying claim to Elizabeth as if he were some primitive potentate. Darcy's conduct might cause Richard to think he had a secret understanding with Elizabeth. But his cousin would know that Bennet had not consented to an engagement since nothing had been mentioned during the frantic search for Elizabeth.

At least he could count on Richard not to gossip about the irregular way Darcy was conducting his affairs. It was all a matter of formality anyway. Once Elizabeth was in her right mind, Darcy could establish an understanding with her. And since he would be staying at Longbourn—he had no intention of letting her out of his sight again—it would be the work of a moment to secure Bennet's consent. He would simply have to face his family's wrath when it came.

The most pressing problem now was preventing the necromancer from attempting to kill Elizabeth—again.

***

When Elizabeth awoke alone in the room she shared with Jane, she had no idea how she had come to be there or how long she had been asleep. The last thing she remembered was Mr. Darcy carrying her in the Old Forest. What had happened since then? Had they questioned Mr. Wickham? Did they know the necromancer's identity? Where was Mr. Darcy?

When she sat up, her head spun, and she had to wait for the moment to pass. She attempted to stand, but she wobbled on her feet and bumped into the bedside table, causing a loud clatter as the candleholder fell over. Instantly, the door sprang open, and Mr. Darcy strode in, alert for any danger. His shoulders relaxed when he saw her. "Why are you out of bed? You should have rung the bell for help!"

Elizabeth settled back on the bed—secretly pleased with an excuse not to move—but she was a bit piqued at his tone. "Mr. Darcy, what are you doing in my sick room? This is most improper!"

His brow furrowed, as if this perfectly natural thought had not occurred to him. "You were in my sick room."

"I was helping you to heal," she said primly. "Have you developed some hitherto unknown healing powers?"

"No."

"Why are you even in attendance at Longbourn?"

His reply was a bit sheepish. "I have been guarding your door."

"I beg your pardon?"

He straightened his shoulders. "The necromancer made an attempt on your life. I do not intend to give him another opportunity."

"So you have appointed yourself my bodyguard?" She laughed incredulously. "Have you been sleeping across my doorway with a naked sword by your side?"

He glanced away uncomfortably. "I do not have a sword."

He does not deny sleeping across my doorway. Elizabeth stared at him. She was the daughter of a minor country gentleman. It was incredible that anyone wanted to abduct her, and even more incredible that anyone of consequence thought her worth saving. Although she supposed Mr. Darcy must be grateful for her saving his life. Perhaps he was merely returning the favor. Yes, he had professed admiration for her, but he had also explained that he could not act on those feelings.

"Surely that is not necessary," she said.

He grimaced. "England once had three vivomancers. The other two are…The necromancer murdered the other two when he realized they could destroy his wights." Elizabeth's hand flew to her mouth. "Your skills are of value to the entire country."

She blinked several times. "That is so hard to credit.…"

"Believe it. The Agency's director is eager to meet you and has tasked me with keeping you safe."

"I doubt he specified sleeping in my doorway," Elizabeth teased.

"No." He moved closer to the bed, a serious expression on his face. "Elizabeth, there is something I must discuss with you—"

Lydia barreled into the room. "I told you she was awake!" she said over her shoulder as Kitty followed her in.

"If I was not before, that entrance would have awakened me," Elizabeth joked.

Not even blinking at Mr. Darcy's presence, Lydia flounced to the end of Elizabeth's bed and took a seat. "Lizzy, you should have accepted Mr. Collins's proposal!"

"Why is that?"

"Then he would not have proposed to me! He sang some dreadful Irish jig! The tune was pleasant enough, but his singing—" She cringed.

Elizabeth smiled sympathetically. "I thought Kitty to be next in line for that 'honor.'"

"I was," Kitty said, wrinkling her nose. "*My* offer was set to an operatic aria. He was unable to hit the high notes…or the low ones."

"So all of the Bennet sisters have refused him?"

"Except for Jane, but Mr. Collins is too in awe of Mr. Bingley to prevail upon her," Lydia said.

"What will the poor man do now?"

Kitty shrugged. "He somehow wrangled an invitation to dinner at Lucas Lodge. They have a plentiful supply of daughters."

"I believe Charlotte is tone deaf," Elizabeth mused.

"A match made in heaven!" Kitty giggled.

"Mama must be exceedingly unhappy," Elizabeth said.

Lydia nodded. "She says all of us have been a trial for her poor nerves, except for you." She slid an oblique look at Mr. Darcy.

"I would think being kidnapped would have been quite a trial for her," Elizabeth said.

Lydia bounced on the mattress. "It was, but all is forgiven now, of course."

This was very perplexing. Elizabeth could not imagine her mother forgiving anything, especially something as reckless as being the victim of a kidnapping. "Why would—?"

But then her mother herself swept into the room. "Lizzy, I am pleased you are well again!"

"I would not say I am entirely—"

Mrs. Bennet simply continued to talk. "Doesn't she look well today, Mr. Darcy?" Elizabeth stared. Her mother had never directed his attention to her before.

Mr. Darcy had sidled toward the door. "She does indeed." His voice was a low murmur. "Perhaps I will visit the kitchen to obtain some food for Elizabeth."

She could not blame him for desiring to escape. Her bedchamber was particularly crowded with the addition of her mother—whose approbation was nearly as alarming as her disapproval.

"Pish!" her mother exclaimed. "Kitty and Lydia can do that! It is certainly not something we would ask of guests." She glared at her youngest daughters until they sullenly slunk from the room.

"I must speak with my cousin," Mr. Darcy added hastily. "I might as well combine the two errands." He gave them a brief nod and slipped through the door. Mr. Darcy was fetching food; her mother was pleased with Elizabeth. Had she awoken in some mirror version of Longbourn?

Her mother took a chair by the bedside as if settling in for a chat. *Argh. My head aches, and I am bone-weary. All I want is some tea and a nap.*

Still, Elizabeth was a bit curious about what had occasioned her mother's sudden approval.

"Miss Lizzy, you are a sly one," her mother said with a knowing smile. "Keeping this to yourself."

Keeping what? Elizabeth guessed at the first thing that made sense. "I speculated about who Mr. Darcy works for, but he never confirmed anything."

Her mother waved that away. "Who cares about that?" She leaned forward and lowered her voice. "I am talking about…the engagement."

Now Elizabeth was thoroughly confused. Who was engaged? "Did Mr. Bingley propose to Jane? I assure you I do not know—"

"No, no!" Her mother flapped her hands in irritation. "I am speaking about your understanding with Mr. Darcy. Just imagine! Ten thousand a year!"

Perhaps I myself have slipped through the mirror. There had been a glorious but furtive kiss in the garden. He had carried her in the Old Forest. Yes, Elizabeth had suffered a blow to the head, but surely she would recollect a proposal. "Mama, I assure you I have no understanding with Mr. Darcy."

"You would not believe how he has been behaving! Guarding you night and day. Insisting that he should be the one to take care of you."

Her mother had not been present when Mr. Darcy all but informed her that he could not marry beneath him. "He is only doing that to protect me. The Council is anxious the necromancer might attack me."

Mrs. Bennet waved that away as unimportant. "That is simply his excuse. He and your father have already started informal discussions for the terms of your marriage contract."

Elizabeth studied the words in her mind, but they still did not make sense. "I beg your pardon?"

"Oh yes!" her mother said gaily, oblivious to Elizabeth's confusion. "Apparently Mr. Darcy is quite generous."

Elizabeth endeavored to calm her breathing and avoid the impulse to shout at her mother, who was, after all, not the author of this situation. Finally, she inquired, "Mama, could you summon Mr. Darcy back here? I would like to speak with him." She discovered she was not nearly so tired as she had been only minutes before.

Her mother stood. "Certainly. But be sure to accommodate and please him. The contract isn't signed yet!"

While her mother summoned Mr. Darcy, Elizabeth rose from her bed and pulled on a dressing gown—armoring herself for the discourse. Although she immediately needed to return to bed. She would have preferred to be fully dressed, but simply did not have the energy.

Mr. Darcy entered a bit warily. As well he might. He set a tray with cold meat, bread, and tea on the table by her bedside.

"My mother is under the impression that you and I have an understanding," Elizabeth said without preamble. "What might have given her that idea?"

Mr. Darcy colored and sat in the chair beside the bed, giving every appearance of collecting his thoughts. He cleared his throat. "I refused to be parted from you. You require protection. And your family, understandably, would not permit me to remove you to Netherfield. I may have *implied* a secret understanding as a means of securing access to ensure your safety."

She was familiar by now with how he left things unsaid.

"My mother related that you and my father discussed the terms of the marriage contract. That is far more than implying an understanding."

He was looking everywhere but at her. "No agreements were reached. He merely inquired what I might have to offer my future wife and appeared satisfied with my answer."

Anger rose through her body like a tide. Slipping from the bed, Elizabeth advanced on him. "Mr. Darcy, marriage agreements do not arise in casual conversation. I am not stupid. I do not recommend that you treat me as if I were—if you ever plan to speak with me again."

He went quite still as he recognized the ice in her tone. "Forgive me, Elizabeth. I know you are not stupid," he finally said in a low voice. "I would not contemplate marrying you for one second if you were."

"But recently you told me that my family's position was too far beneath your own for you to contemplate making an offer."

"Yesterday I was a fool!" he said viciously.

What could possibly account for such an abrupt change of heart? "Do you believe you have compromised me?" she asked. "Because I assure you that my family will not hold you to—"

"I almost lost you!" he cried.

Surprise rocked her back on her heels.

"I almost lost you," he repeated. "For hours I knew not where you were or if Wickham had killed you. I realized nothing could compare to the pain of not having you in my life. I am desperately in love with you. I have loved you almost since the first moments of our acquaintance."

Elizabeth's breath caught. "But your family—"

"My family can go hang!" Her mouth dropped open. "Georgiana and Richard will love you," he continued in a softer tone. "If the others do not, I care not."

He had handed her his still-beating heart, and she appreciated how vulnerable he allowed himself to be. But the discussion remained...unbalanced.

"I am honored by your admiration," she began. His head jerked up as he recognized the shift in her tone. "But you talk as if *yours* is the only opinion that matters."

His eyes were round and horrified. "W-Would you refuse me?"

"I have not been asked."

He rubbed a hand over his chin, "To be fair, I did intend to make an offer—just not within minutes of your awaking from a head injury."

She nodded. "Understandable."

"However, I did not anticipate your mother's immediately pressing the issue."

Her mouth quirked upward. "A strategic error."

He smiled ruefully. "Apparently." He blinked once. Twice. "I must admit I did not give much consideration to the idea that you might refuse. My fortune. My family's position. I have much to offer a wife."

She regarded him sardonically. "You claim to know me. What do you think I would value from a marital union?"

The realization dawned on his face. "Love." He made a choked noise. Had it never occurred to him that she might not love him? Did all wealthy men believe all women were destined to fall in love with them? "Elizabeth, I love you most ardently….Do you love me?" The apprehension on his face was difficult to watch. She could not bear to draw the moment out.

"Yes. I do."

He slumped in relief. "Then—" He moved to position himself on one knee. "Elizabeth, will you—"

Chapter Twelve

"No." She held out a hand.

"No?"

"I am rather put out with you at the moment and would prefer not to answer any questions…any important questions wearing a dressing gown in a sick room. And I believe you should not commit yourself to such a course following a great threat to my life. You might regret it later."

He glanced down at the floor and then back at her. "That is…fair. These are not the most auspicious circumstances for such momentous decisions. I know I will not change my mind, but I am willing to wait and prove it to you. Will you make me one promise?"

"Perhaps."

"Will you promise not to accept another man's offer of marriage until I have the opportunity to make one?"

She laughed. "Who do you think might make me an offer?"

The corners of his mouth curved upward. "Mr. Collins is still unattached."

Her laughter increased. "Yes, I promise I will not accept another man's offer of marriage without first listening to your proposal."

"Then I am satisfied—for the moment."

***

Leaving Elizabeth alone for any length of time made Darcy anxious, although he knew he was being irrational. Longbourn was warded by her father's mancy, but he could still imagine any number of ways a clever villain could gain access to her room.

He was suitably chastened by her rebuke. She was absolutely correct; he had not considered her feelings at all. He had assumed she felt about him the same way he felt about her, and that his wealth would compensate for any inequality in their affections for each other. But he knew her better than that. Only love would tempt her, not wealth. Thank goodness he had won her love; for an awful moment he had worried she would tell him she could not love him. He should know better than to make assumptions when it came to Elizabeth Bennet.

He had hoped to sweep her off her feet with a romantic proposal. But he would have to wait for a future opportunity.

Darcy would have preferred to spend the whole day by Elizabeth's side, but he had other urgent concerns to address. He reluctantly made his way to one of Longbourn's drawing rooms, where Richard awaited him. "How does Miss Elizabeth fare?" his cousin inquired.

"She is sleeping again," he replied. "But I believe she is recovering quickly."

Richard's expression was grim. "I just received a note from Colonel Forster. Wickham has escaped."

Darcy uttered an oath.

"Just so," Richard agreed. "It appears he had help. My guess is the necromancer is scheming to employ his talents again."

"We must conceal Elizabeth."

Richard nodded. "I have been considering our next move. We cannot remain here indefinitely. Even if Wickham himself does not seek her out, Miss Elizabeth is too easy for the necromancer to find."

"Perhaps I should remove her to Netherfield."

"That would do her reputation no favors," Richard pointed out. "It is also the second place they would look for her."

Darcy rubbed the back of his neck. Richard was not wrong. "I could take her to Darcy House or Pemberley." The idea was immediately appealing to Darcy. Hours alone with Elizabeth? It would be heavenly.

Richard raised a skeptical eyebrow.

"We would be accompanied by a suitable chaperone!" Darcy said quickly.

"I am sure," Richard murmured. "As delightful as it would be for you, the necromancer would quickly guess those locations. We must also determine how he knows she is a vivomancer. If we can answer that question, we may be able to identify him."

"You have kept Cranston apprised of recent events. No doubt he will be investigating that question."

"Of course," Richard said slowly. "But that may not be sufficient...if the leak is internal to the Agency...."

Darcy regarded his cousin as something niggled at the back of his mind. What was Richard thinking? "You suspect the director might be the necromancer!"

Richard's expression was pained. "I do not want to credit the idea, but the pieces fit. He is one of the few people with knowledge of Miss Elizabeth's abilities. And I gave Cranston the list of the necromancer's followers. He has not moved against any of them. That may be for political reasons, but...."

Darcy rubbed his chin, considering the awful possibility. The investigation into the necromancer had been instigated by Richard based on rumors he had heard. Once Darcy had learned the scope of the Necromancer's activities, he had been amazed the Agency had not heard such rumors before. Perhaps there was a reason for a lack of previous investigation.

The thought threatened to choke him. If the very heart of the Agency was corrupt, what hope did they have? Nobody else was likely to suspect the director, let alone investigate him. He and Richard could tell nobody of their suspicions until they were confirmed.

"What do you propose?" he asked his cousin.

"You and I should return to town and visit Cranston. We can learn more by speaking with him."

"But I do not want Elizabeth to be unprotected," Darcy said.

"Perhaps..." Richard said. "My mother could take her in for a few days. That would also alleviate any concerns about propriety. Matlock House is well protected. My father has paid a fortune for wards."

Darcy rubbed his chin as he considered the idea. His aunt and uncle would be shocked when he announced his engagement to Elizabeth. But as of yet there was nothing to announce. It might soften the blow if they made her acquaintance beforehand. He doubted he might ever win his uncle's approval; the man thought very highly of the ties of blood and family. But his aunt might eventually be charmed by Elizabeth's wit and manners. Certainly it would not hurt for them to make her acquaintance. Elizabeth exhibited curiosity about London and would probably consent to the journey.

"It is a good thought, Richard," he said. "Will you send a message to your mother? I hope Elizabeth will be well enough to travel tomorrow."

***

The next few days were a whirlwind for Elizabeth. Mr. Darcy consulted her about his scheme to remove her to London and the home of the Earl of Matlock, and she readily agreed. She certainly would be better protected there—in Mr. Darcy's company—than at Longbourn. She had visited London little; staying with a peer of the realm promised to be an exciting experience—despite the danger. Her mother was beside herself at the honor that would accrue to her daughter.

Her father, newly awakened to his daughter's mortality, did not desire her to make such a journey accompanied only by gentlemen they barely knew. At first, Mr. Bennet was bent on having the entire family travel with her, but this was not a practical plan. After much discussion, Jane was selected to accompany the party.

Although she was sorry to take Jane away from Mr. Bingley when their relationship was at such a promising stage, Elizabeth was grateful for the company. Her father insisted that the rest of the family would follow no less than a day later and stay with their relatives, the Gardiners, at their house on Gracechurch Street.

The party traveled to London without incident and in great comfort in Mr. Bingley's coach, which he had lent to Mr. Darcy for the occasion. Matlock House was far larger than any London house Elizabeth had ever seen. The butler escorted them into a parlor lavishly decorated with blue silk curtains and gilt furnishings. Lady Margaret rose to embrace her son and nephew—after which Colonel Fitzwilliam made the introductions.

Lady Margaret's welcome to the Bennet sisters was gracious if not particularly warm. She cordially invited them to sit, and a maid provided tea and biscuits—precisely as one ought to treat guests. She inquired about their families, quickly establishing that they had no acquaintances in common.

The countess then turned her attention to Colonel Fitzwilliam. "Did you know that the Duke of Burlingham's second son is engaged to Viscount Fortunegate's daughter?"

"No, I had not heard."

She nodded. "An extremely advantageous match on both sides."

"Indeed."

Elizabeth did not imagine that the topic of marriages was a random one.

Lady Margaret's gaze fixed on Mr. Darcy. "The Earl of Mansfield's daughter made her bow this year. Such a lovely girl! Have you met her?"

"I have not had that pleasure," he said in a measured tone.

"The marital season is well underway!" she exclaimed. "You should remain in London rather than traipsing around the country. Pemberley needs an heir."

He set his teacup on the table. "A certain amount of traipsing has been necessary for Council business." Mr. Darcy had informed Elizabeth in the carriage that his aunt and uncle knew about his position with the Agency.

Lady Margaret waved her hand negligently. "Someone else can perform those duties." Mr. Darcy heaved a sigh and did not reply to a comment he had undoubtedly heard before. "You have an obligation to the Darcy name," his aunt insisted as her gaze slid over Elizabeth and Jane. She must worry they had designs on her son and nephew.

A contrary impulse struck Elizabeth. *I could request my proposal from Mr. Darcy now.* He was certainly eager to offer it. How shocked Lady Margaret would be to discover that *Elizabeth* was the one preventing the banns from being posted. *But,* she reminded herself, *the object of the visit is to catch the necromancer. Shocking Lady Margaret must wait for another day.*

The Earl of Matlock was not at home when they arrived, but his presence was promised for dinner. Lord John, the earl's heir and Richard's older brother, was at the family's country estate—where Mr. Darcy's sister Georgiana also resided—so they did not expect to encounter him.

Fortunately, their audience with Lady Margaret was not long. Elizabeth was quite relieved to adjourn to her bedchamber for an hour of rest before she prepared herself for dinner.

***

By the end of dinner Elizabeth found herself wishing that Lady Margaret's cold formality was the worst trial she had to face; the Earl of Matlock was far worse. He regarded Elizabeth in particular with an appraising eye when they were introduced, perhaps wondering if she was angling after his son?

During the meal he barely acknowledged the Bennet sisters. Instead, he regaled his son and nephew with stories from the House of Lords and complaints about how the Council was setting policies on magical use.

Elizabeth had encountered his sort before. He believed his wealth and position exempted him from the usual constraints of good manners. No doubt another contributor to his impoliteness was the wine glass by his elbow, which a footman was careful to keep full.

Near the end of the meal, the earl asked Mr. Darcy, "Why were you in Hertfordshire of all places when Richard needed to rescue you?"

Colonel Fitzwilliam chuckled. "He hardly needed rescuing, Papa."

The earl remained focused on his nephew. "Why were you consorting with the local rustics?" he asked with a sloppy sneer.

Mr. Darcy's face went very still, wiped of all expression. After a moment, he said, "I will allow Miss Elizabeth to tell that story. I am certain it is most amusing from her perspective."

The earl scowled, but Elizabeth gave Mr. Darcy an appreciative smile. "I do not know all the particulars, but my sister Jane and I found Mr. Darcy floating in the River Lea along a part of the shore that belongs to my family's estate." That would remind the earl that she was a gentleman's daughter.

"My goodness!" the countess exclaimed.

"It is my understanding that he had been on some Agency business that went awry."

"Very badly awry," Mr. Darcy agreed.

"Jane and I pulled him from the river. I helped restart his breathing. Then my father and his footman took him to the house."

Lady Margaret's eyes were round with amazement as she realized how close she had come to losing her nephew. "Thank God!"

"Yes, yes, quite fortunate." The earl gestured with his wine glass. "You must have thanked providence that a man of such fortune arrived at your family's doorstep."

The colonel rolled his eyes, and Mr. Darcy opened his mouth to object, but Elizabeth spoke first. "We thanked God for his life—as we would for *anyone's* life." A disgruntled expression passed over the earl's face at the rebuke. "We were pleased to welcome him to our home and help him recover. For the entirety of his stay with us, we thought he was a wool merchant from London."

"It was necessary to conceal my presence since I had reason to believe the enemy was searching for me," Mr. Darcy explained.

"A wool merchant!" The earl laughed raucously, slapping the table with his open palm. "Imagine that! Darcy: a wool merchant." The countess tittered a bit, but the others sat in a strained silence.

"I was impressed that he was well-read and well-mannered for a wool merchant, not to mention extremely knowledgeable about magic." Elizabeth caught Mr. Darcy's eye and was rewarded with a warm look. "It was not until Mr. Bingley arrived in Hertfordshire that my family learned Mr. Darcy's true name."

The earl waggled a finger at her. "So that is when you baited your hook for him? Eh? Or were you content with a mere wool merchant? I suppose beggars cannot be choosers."

Mr. Darcy gasped, and Elizabeth felt her face flush, but the earl continued—pointing to Jane. "And, I suppose you have set your cap for Richard here." He indicated his youngest son with a jerk of his chin. "But I warn you, like Darcy, he must marry an heiress of good breeding. My eldest, Edward, disgraced the family name, and we cannot afford another scandal." He gestured expansively to both women, slurring his words. "So you must go fishing in other ponds." He laughed raucously, a hollow sound in the silent room.

The countess stood abruptly and gave a signal to a footman. "Walter, that is quite enough. It is past time for you to retire." He regarded her belligerently for a moment but then shrugged and slumped in his chair.

The footman pulled the earl's chair from the table. Then he and another footman helped the earl to his feet in what was clearly a practiced routine. He muttered under his breath as he stumbled from the room but did not object.

Mr. Darcy's eyes widened as he followed these proceedings, but the colonel's expression was resigned. Lady Margaret's face was pale but composed as she resumed her seat. She took a long gulp of wine, set down the cup, and turned to her son. "Do you believe it will rain tomorrow?"

***

Following that disastrous dinner, Darcy experienced no compunction about escorting Elizabeth to her assigned bedchamber. Let his aunt construe his actions as she wished. He would rejoin the others for a ritual of cards and conversation following the meal, but he indulged himself to steal a few minutes with Elizabeth when she pleaded fatigue and announced she would retire early.

When he recalled how his uncle had embarrassed Elizabeth, Darcy's cheeks burned with shame. He had needed to restrain an impulse to strike the man. In a whispered aside, Richard had said his father's drinking had recently grown worse, but even he had never witnessed such crass behavior.

Now he and Elizabeth stood in the entrance to her bedchamber, oddly reluctant to part even for one night.

"I must apologize for my uncle's words…and conduct," he said.

"I do not hold you accountable for your family's behavior. You do not hold me accountable for mine." A smile briefly appeared on her lips.

"I have never witnessed anyone in your family behave in a deliberately cruel way. And my uncle is an earl. He should adhere to a higher standard. He believes he has superior manners."

"What did he mean when he mentioned his son Edward?"

Darcy blew out a breath. It was a difficult subject. "Two years ago, my cousin Edward was executed by the Council for the use of dark magic."

Elizabeth gasped. "Executed! How terrible."

Darcy closed his eyes briefly. It had been a difficult time for the entire family, and he did not want to remember it. "Edward had been his parents' favorite and excessively indulged. They were blind to his wanton and cruel behavior. Richard and I were saddened but not astonished that he turned to dark magic; he was a bully to us when we were children."

"Surely such executions are rare!"

"Indeed. The Council prefers imprisonment. But they found that Edward had murdered another man with his pyromancy." While mancy could be used in self-defense or for law enforcement activities, the penalty for murder with magic was death. "It was a dispute over a gambling debt. Even then my uncle might have convinced them to give a sentence of life in prison. However, Edward killed someone else in an attempt to conceal the first murder. The Council captured him, put him on trial, and condemned him to death."

"That must have been devastating for the family."

"Yes. The Council kept the affair out of the papers, but everyone in the *ton* knew. My aunt was a ghost of herself for a long time; only recently has she ventured out in society again. My uncle never speaks about the business, but he imbibes excessively."

"This is why you need to marry a woman of good breeding."

"Indeed, particularly after my father's…misbehavior." Following Edward's execution, his aunt had cried herself dry. His uncle had been practically a sleepwalker. John had avoided London, leaving the others to shoulder the burden.

"Since Richard and I are the only unmarried men in the family, my aunt and uncle believe that our marriages are necessary to restore the family honor. But recently I realized that it should not be my responsibility." He regarded her solemnly. "It is far more important to follow the dictates of my heart."

"Of course," she murmured with her eyes downcast.

"I beg you not to take my uncle's words to heart," Darcy said. "I do not credit them, nor do my friends and family."

Her laugh was bitter. "You did not want to marry me because of such sentiments. Surely they will follow me if I choose to enter your world."

The doubt in her voice sent anxiety creeping through Darcy. He had believed she would accept his proposal eventually. *We have an understanding. It is only a matter of time.* But he could not dismiss her doubts. Some in his circle would view Elizabeth as beneath them, and he could not prevent that.

He reached out and pulled her toward him, enfolding her in his embrace. "I will do my best to protect you. You will always be loved."

Her stiff body relaxed against his as she rested her head upon his chest—a good sign. He delicately stroked her curls with his fingertips. "Perhaps the situation will appear less hopeless in the morning." She sighed and nuzzled his chest.

His breath caught as her actions triggered unexpected feelings throughout his body. "You are still recovering from the blow to your head. Of course you are fatigued. But tomorrow you may sleep as long as you would like. My uncle's house will be safe; he has purchased many magical protections. Naturally, I will return to guard your door later in the evening."

"It is not all necessary. Your back must be quite tender after so many nights on the floor."

"I will not risk losing you again."

"What will your aunt and uncle think when you position yourself across my doorway?"

"They will think I am quite devoted to the well-being of the woman who saved my life. Which I am." He took her hand and gently kissed the back.

"Surely they will guess your feelings run deeper."

"They already suspect—which is good. They might as well accustom themselves to the idea." He turned her hand over and daringly kissed her palm.

She shuddered. "You are a dangerous man."

He gave her a wicked grin. "Of course, my preference would be to guard you from *within* your room, but my aunt and uncle would be scandalized."

Her eyes widened in shock. "Mr. Darcy!"

"Please call me William."

"Perhaps I should not if you speak so scandalously." She laughed.

"It is not only my speech that is scandalous." He could restrain himself no longer. His lips descended on hers for a searing kiss. Nothing else existed but the pleasure of her lips and her warm body pressing against his. He longed to exist in this moment forever. Suspended in time. Two pairs of lips touching. Two bodies perpetually intertwined.

Unfortunately, Darcy's body was enjoying the sensations a bit too much. He pulled back and stepped away from her, immediately regretting the loss of her warmth. "I must cease now while I can still call myself a gentleman." He took a moment to get his ragged breathing back under control. "Richard and I will likely be away—visiting the director—before you awake," he said.

"I should go with you. Vivomancy may be the only power that can fight necromancy."

"If Cranston is the one hunting you, the last thing we should do is take you to him. We hope to learn the truth during our visit. Fortunately, he is not likely to start a fight in the Council building."

She pressed both of her hands on the front of his jacket. "Please be careful."

He could not help but be touched by her concern. "I will. I promise." She was swaying on her feet. "You should sleep. Good night, Elizabeth."

"Good night, Mr. D—William."

He watched until the door closed behind her—and the lock clicked.

***

Despite the seriousness of the situation, Darcy was in good spirits as he and Richard rode out the next morning. Elizabeth was as safe as possible, and she apparently viewed his courtship ever more favorably. At times he had despaired they would ever reach that point.

However, as he and Richard grew closer to the Council complex, his mood grew more somber. Richard, who had worked with the Agency's director, Viscount Cranston, far more closely, was downright grim. Finally, he said, "Darcy, we cannot simply waltz into the ministry and accuse the director of being a necromancer! That would be foolish as well as rude."

"That was not my plan," Darcy responded calmly. "I thought I would ask some questions and you could use your verimancy to determine whether he is telling the truth."

Richard frowned. "He knows about my magic. He will not attempt to lie in my presence."

"Evasive answers will give us useful information as well," Darcy noted. "Leave the questions to me. Just signal to me if he is telling the truth."

"And if he is the necromancer, what are we to do? He might attack us if he realizes we guess the truth."

"He cannot summon wights during the day," Darcy reminded his cousin. "The Council building is full of mancers. Striking at us would be inadvisable. If he does, we can summon many other mages to help us."

"I can conceive of many flaws in this purported 'plan' of yours," Richard grumbled.

Darcy sighed. "No doubt. But we do not have the luxury of time to devise a better strategy."

His cousin nodded a weary acknowledgement and led the way through the gates into the Council complex. Darcy could only hope they were not being foolhardy in confronting a dark magic practitioner this way. Perhaps they should have recruited others to help. Well, it was too late now.

Chapter Thirteen

The Council building itself was an ornate gothic structure in the heart of Westminster with a spectacular view of the Thames. The Agency inhabited a squat structure that had been constructed hastily over an ancient alleyway. The utilitarian addition to the main building was a bit of an eyesore, but some of the offices did provide glimpses of the river.

Richard and Darcy waited for half an hour in the director's outer chamber before being admitted to his office. Cranston was a tall man in his early fifties, athletic, and quick to smile. "Darcy, Fitzwilliam." He shook their hands while peering behind them. "You did not bring the vivomancer?"

Darcy stiffened. "We were not sure of her safety."

Cranston frowned as he motioned them to the chairs opposite his desk. Richard took the far seat where he would not be in the director's line of sight. "Surely the Council building is the safest place for her. Is she really so timid a creature?"

Darcy bristled. "Not in the least. I am loath to bring her into danger." From the corner of his eye, he noticed Richard casting a discreet truth field over the room. Fortunately, Cranston's attention was on Darcy.

Cranston made a placating motion. "Understandable given Wickham's actions, but we are now on our guard. She should be perfectly safe here. It is her duty to serve Britain…although women do not perceive duty and honor as we do."

Darcy had never disliked the director before, but today every one of the man's utterances made his skin crawl. "I assure you that she has a strong sense of honor—"

"Then is it a matter of ability? It is a shame she was not trained here—"

"She is exceedingly powerful."

Cranston shook his head. "I do not understand where the problem lies. If circumstances arise where she cannot protect herself, the Council's mancers will do so. You know we need her skills to defeat the necromancer."

Darcy leaned forward in his chair. "Before I bring Miss Elizabeth to the Council, I must know who is aware of her identity as a vivomancer."

"Hmm?" Cranston furrowed his brow at the abrupt change of subject.

"I relayed her secret to Richard with the request that you keep it in the utmost confidence—"

"Yes." Cranston looked down at his desk and shuffled some papers. "I do not comprehend the necessity of such a stipulation. Plenty of people have been known as vivomancers throughout history. It is a position of honor. This Bennet woman should be eager to claim the title—"

"That is not your concern!" Darcy thundered. "I expected you to honor my request. Did you do so?"

Cranston wet his lips. "Yes. Yes, of course."

Darcy was not reassured, but when he slid his eyes to Richard, his cousin gave a slight nod. Cranston was speaking the truth as he understood it. Of course, his idea of "utmost confidence" might not be the same as Darcy's.

"Who did you tell?"

"I do not understand how that is relevant—"

"Somehow the necromancer learned that Elizabeth was a vivomancer and sent Wickham to abduct her," Darcy said in a low voice. "I know that *I* did not tell him. Nor did Richard."

Cranston colored. "And you believe *I* did? I would never violate a trust! I am a man of my word!"

Richard nodded again. Darcy relaxed slightly. But Cranston's denial did not completely exclude him from suspicion.

"You do not practice necromancy?"

"Of course not!" Cranston's face was practically purple.

"Truth," Richard said.

"And you are not working with the necromancer?"

Cranston shot to his feet. "How dare you—!"

Darcy stood and faced him. "Answer the question! Do you work with the necromancer?"

"No."

Richard cleared his throat. "Truth."

Darcy slumped back into his chair. Cranston was not the blackguard they were seeking.

"You have been truth-reading me the whole time?" Cranston snarled at Richard.

Richard gave the man a conciliatory shrug, but Darcy was unapologetic. "The necromancer learned about Elizabeth's vivomancy somehow. You are an obvious source."

Cranston pulled a handkerchief from his pocket and mopped his brow. "And you believed I might be the necromancer?"

"It is likely to be someone affiliated with the Council," Richard noted. "Her life was not in danger until the Council knew her identity."

Cranston fell back into his chair. "I suspected we had a leak...I thought one of the staff might...but they did not know about Miss Bennet...."

"Did you inform everyone on the Council about Elizabeth's vivomancy?" Darcy inquired.

"Of course not. We could never maintain secrecy if so many people knew." Cranston rubbed his chin thoughtfully. "I told Sir Lloyd...."

Darcy nodded. The leader of the Council was at least 80 years of age, too old to be the necromancer.

"And Lady Farha...."

"The necromancer is definitely male, but perhaps she is lending him assistance?"

Richard and Cranston both shook their heads. "Her son was killed on the peninsula by one of Napoleon's necromancers. She hates them," the director said.

Cranston worried the cuff of his jacket as he mused. "I do not believe I told anyone else."

Richard nodded to Darcy. Cranston was telling the truth as he knew it. Darcy slouched into his chair. How had the necromancer learned Elizabeth's identity if not from the Council? They could visit Sir Lloyd and Lady Farha. Perhaps they had told someone....

Cranston snapped his fingers. "There was someone else! But surely he would not—" The man's eyes darted to Richard.

"Who is it?" Darcy demanded.

"I am sure it is nothing. I believed we were alone when I related the information to Sir Lloyd and Lady Farha. Afterward I spied him outside the door. But he is a Council member in good standing—!"

"Who do you mean?" Darcy asked impatiently.

"He is a peer of the realm!"

Darcy surged to his feet and stared down at Cranston. "Who. Did. You. Tell?"

Cranston's eyes fixed on Richard. "Your father. The Earl of Matlock."

Richard started so violently that he almost tipped over his chair.

A black pit opened in Darcy's stomach. He had been prepared for anything—anything except hearing the name of a relative. No, surely it meant nothing.

Richard stared at Cranston in a daze.

"It means little," Darcy said hastily. "Possibly Uncle Walter passed the information along to the wrong person. Surely if he were practicing necromancy, you would know."

"Of course." Cranston bobbed his head in agreement.

Richard said nothing for a long moment. Then he spoke slowly with an odd detachment in his voice. "My father has been from home frequently as of late. I do not always know why he travels or who he associates with."

Darcy regarded him sharply. "Where has he gone?"

"I do not always know, although…." Richard's head jerked in Darcy's direction. "Good Lord! He was in Bedfordshire when you were! He was visiting Viscount Waring. I thought nothing of it at the time." Darcy's cousin was as white as a sheet.

"But-But, your father is a member. He supports the Council!" Cranston asserted.

"Certainly. In most things." Richard shook his head. "However, in private—particularly when he is in his cups—he berates the Council and their narrow-minded views of acceptable magic. Particularly after Edward's…I never paid much heed."

"He still blames them for his son's death," Cranston murmured. "And he was among the Council members who voted against arresting the necromancer's followers on Darcy's list."

Richard swore.

"But the earl is a terramancer, not a necromancer," Darcy said.

Cranston cast an eye at the wall of books on one side of his office. "John Barnabas wrote in the 1700s that any mancer could turn into a necromancer with the proper rituals and…sacrifices."

"What sort of sacrifices—? No, I do not want to know." Darcy uttered several oaths.

"It is possible your father found such a ritual," Cranston said. "He always was curious about the darker sides of magic—ideas that others shied away from."

Darcy's eyes widened. "When I first encountered the necromancer, he was urging his followers to abandon their fear of dark magic."

Richard shook his head. "I do not want to believe it, but if there is any chance my father is the blackguard we seek, we are in deep trouble."

Darcy jumped to his feet. "And I left Elizabeth at his house!"

***

Elizabeth descended to breakfast at Matlock House alone. Jane was suffering from a minor cold; Elizabeth had alleviated the symptoms to the best of her ability and arranged to send a tray to her sister's room. William and his cousin had departed for the Council building early that morning. At the breakfast table, Elizabeth encountered Lady Margaret, who was excessively chatty—perhaps endeavoring to compensate for her husband's rudeness the previous evening.

Elizabeth was halfway through her toast and coffee when the earl joined them, red-eyed and sluggish from the wine he had consumed the night before. Perhaps his sore head also accounted for why he glowered at Elizabeth, or perhaps it was simply his presumption that she was chasing after his nephew. Explaining how his nephew was actually chasing *her* would not likely improve the man's mood.

Eventually, even Lady Margaret's cheerful chatter faltered in the face of her husband's ill humor, and the table fell silent. As soon as she could, Elizabeth excused herself. Escaping the house would be preferable, but she had promised William not to venture out alone. She could only hope that he and his cousin would return soon.

As she ascended the stairs, Elizabeth considered whether it was warm enough to read in the garden, which would surely be safe enough enclosed by walls. She had reached the top step when she became aware of an unsettling sensation—as if ice were sliding down her spine. Something was profoundly wrong, and it was magical in origin. Her flesh crawled. What could possibly create this creepy, out-of-joint feeling?

Elizabeth could not afford to ignore this wrongness. Her sister was in the house. Colonel Fitzwilliam and William would be returning here. And the Matlock family and their servants lived here. Had some evil entered their home? She considered requesting the earl's assistance but dismissed the idea immediately. He would undoubtedly scoff if she could report nothing more than a sense of uneasiness.

Perhaps if she could identify the source of the wrongness....

The disturbing sensation definitely emanated from the second story. She had not noticed it on the first floor. Elizabeth followed the feeling down the hallway, past the door to her bedchamber and past Jane's—then past doors that surely led to other guest chambers.

The sense of wrongness grew, raising the hairs on the back of her neck. Her nerves screamed to run away; nothing good could come from continuing. The sensation was vaguely reminiscent of those from the wight attack, but wights could not possibly manifest during the day. What could this be?

The only door remaining was at the end of the hallway. Unlike the others, this door was slightly ajar. Perhaps that was allowing the profound wrongness to escape. Elizabeth was sure the door had been closed previously.

She hesitated. Entering the room was a violation of her hosts' privacy. The door might have been left ajar by a maid. What if the chamber was revealed to be Lord Walter's dressing room?

But the sense of wrongness was so palpable that she could not ignore it. Surely whatever was in there presented a danger to the inhabitants of Matlock House, and she had a duty to discover it. Elizabeth pushed the door gently, and it swung open with a creak that caused her to wince.

Sunlight streamed in from windows on two sides of a chamber that was richly decorated with brocade and blue velvet. No expense had been spared. The enormous bed was covered by a canopy embroidered with gold thread. It could have been the earl's bedchamber save for the figure lying on the bed.

Elizabeth stumbled to a halt. Had she interrupted someone's sleep? A second glance told her the person was not asleep. The man's pose was formal and rigid. His legs were straight, and his hands were folded over his chest like a...like a corpse.

He was dressed richly and formally—in finely tailored clothes complete with a pocket watch, intricately folded cravat, and hessian boots. He was a handsome man, with brown hair brushed back from his face. Elizabeth detected a resemblance to Colonel Fitzwilliam and his father.

Stifling a cry of surprise, she crept closer to the bed, noticing the waxiness of the man's features and the dust collected on his clothes. Good heavens! She must be gazing upon a wax version of the Matlocks' dead son! How very disturbing. She had read about exhibits of wax figures traveling the country. A wax figure of a specific individual would be exorbitantly expensive.

But the more Elizabeth stared at the figure, the more she wondered at its composition. It did not resemble wax. Despite being inanimate, the body appeared to be composed of human flesh.

No, it must be wax. The alternative was unthinkable.

But she had to know.

Elizabeth reached out a finger and touched the man's hand. It yielded to the touch like flesh, even showing a slight change of color from the press of her finger. Wax would not do that. The skin was cold to the touch.

Her heart thudding, Elizabeth searched the man's wrist for a pulse and found nothing. His chest did not rise and fall. Her vivomancy detected no spark of life. And yet his body did not decay. How was it preserved? What had happened to that poor man's soul? Did it inhabit a corpse-like body, forever separated from God?

A cold wave of horror washed through her. Now she realized that wrongness for what it was: the magical residue of necromancy. Somehow Edward Fitzwilliam had been suspended between life and death.

The scrape of a shoe on the floor behind her caused Elizabeth to startle and spin around. The earl stood in the open doorway. "Miss Elizabeth, you have anticipated my need for you. This does simplify things." A smile spread over his face. His eyes were still bloodshot, but his face was now animated with a dangerously wild energy.

Fear paralyzed her for a moment as her mind screamed that she must escape, but Lord Walter blocked the only exit. Elizabeth reached out with her magic to defend herself, but there was nothing she could use in the room. No plants or animals. No living matter that would come to her aid.

The earl laughed and made a gesture to someone in the hallway. Several young men burst into the room, filling the space between Elizabeth and the exit. She had originally assumed they were footmen or ruffians, but a second glance told her they were well-dressed and apparently well-bred. She had discovered the necromancer's aristocratic followers—and, if she was not mistaken, the necromancer.

Escape was impossible for the moment, but perhaps she might obtain some information. "Why have you preserved your son's body?" she asked the earl.

The earl raised an eyebrow. "I thought you would have guessed. I intend to bring him back to life."

Elizabeth sucked in a breath. "That is impossible."

He regarded her like a particularly dull child. "No. It is difficult, but not impossible." He stalked toward her. "It is difficult because there are two essential elements that are hard to obtain. The first is the power of a vivomancer. Ironic, isn't it? The life-giving force of vivomancy is exactly what a necromancer needs for this particular task."

"I will never help you!" Elizabeth spat out.

He smiled, showing all his teeth. "Fortunately, I do not require your cooperation; I only require your presence." He stared contemplatively at his son's form on the bed. "I was anxious about how I would gain access to you after Wickham failed, believing it would require a tedious journey to Hertfordshire. But then Darcy obligingly brought you right to my doorstep. I must remember to write him a note expressing my gratitude."

Chills went down Elizabeth's spine. "That is what happened to the other vivomancers. You endeavored to drain their power, and it killed them."

Lord Walter scowled. "Baldwin attempted to fight me and brought his death upon himself. Lady Genevieve proved too old for my needs; when I tested her suitability, her heart gave out. Imagine my delight when I learned there was such a young, ripe vivomancer available. I have high hopes that you might survive…at least until the end of the ceremony."

Elizabeth strove to keep her face impassive so he would not notice how his callous words struck fear in her heart. "What is the other element you need?" she asked, not really caring about the answer. The longer he talked, the more likely it was that William and his cousin might return and rescue her.

"Ah. Bringing someone back to life requires a great deal of energy. Do you know how necromancers power their spells?"

Elizabeth suspected she did, but she shook her head.

"Deaths." The earl savored the word. "I require many deaths. And the deaths of fellow mancers provide the most power. Tonight is the beginning of a new Council season, and all my fellow Council members will assemble for the tedious ceremony we perform every year. It commemorates the founding of the Council in 1503 by John Chadwick, and it is always conducted outside beside the Thames for various stupid historical reasons. But at least today's ceremony will be far more interesting."

"You are insane," Elizabeth said. "You truly believe you can attack and kill the most powerful assembly of mancers in the kingdom?"

He grinned at her. "Miss Elizabeth, you should have more faith in me. I have an army of wights. When they drain magical energy from the

Council mages, I will funnel it into Edward—quite fitting since they are the ones who condemned him to death."

Elizabeth shuddered. What a horrible plan! But the eyes of the earl's followers suggested they were mesmerized by his words. They believed in his scheme and were eager participants.

"Now, we should be on our way before anyone arrives to impede our progress," the earl said smoothly.

Two of his followers had arranged Edward Fitzwilliam's body onto a makeshift litter and one was using mancy to gently float the litter into the air. Everyone watched as it glided through the door and into the hallway.

At the earl's signal, two of his followers seized Elizabeth's arms. *No,* she thought. *I will not let myself be taken to the Council and be used to kill innocent people.* She struggled against her captors, kicking one in the shin and managing a glancing blow on the other man's cheek.

Unperturbed, the earl said, "Now, now. None of that." He touched a hand to her head, and instantly everything went dark.

Chapter Fourteen

Darcy raced into Matlock House, Richard hard on his heels. He nearly collided with Roland the butler after tearing the door open. "Mr. Darcy?" The servant managed to infuse the simple words with a world of disapproval.

"Where is Miss Elizabeth?" Darcy nearly shouted at the man.

"Where is my father?" Richard asked almost simultaneously.

Lady Margaret emerged from a nearby drawing room, embroidery in one hand. "Goodness! What is the matter?"

Darcy looked up the stairs. Should he ensure Elizabeth's safety first, or should he confront his uncle? After all, they could not be certain the earl was the threat.

"What is all this fuss about?" his aunt demanded.

Darcy was in no mood for explanations. "Where is Elizabeth—Miss Elizabeth?"

"I do not know," his aunt responded. "I only recently returned from a visit to Lady Maxwell. Miss Jane Bennet was in bed with a cold. I assumed her sister was keeping her company."

Darcy raced for the stairs, taking them two at a time. The others followed. "Where is Father?" Richard asked as he climbed the stairs.

"How should I know?" Lady Margaret replied. "Perhaps at his club? Business often takes him there."

Darcy strode to Elizabeth's room and pulled open the door without knocking. From the top of the stairs, his aunt gasped at this effrontery. If he startled Elizabeth, Darcy was prepared to happily apologize. But the room was empty. The bed was neatly made, and there was no sign of its occupant.

He made haste to Miss Jane Bennet's room, managing to confine himself to a knock before throwing open the door when she bade him enter.

Fully dressed, Jane sat on the bed with a book in her lap. Her eyes went wide at the sight of Darcy. No doubt his expression was thunderous. He barely managed not to shout. "I apologize for the intrusion, Miss Bennet. I have an urgent need to find your sister. Do you know her whereabouts?"

She frowned. "No. I have not seen her all day. It is passing strange. I took breakfast in my room, but I expected her to join me for luncheon." She hastily clambered off her bed.

Darcy had already pivoted back into the hallway. "Where is Elizabeth?" he demanded from his aunt.

"I have not the slightest idea!" She sounded bewildered. "She joined us for breakfast, but since then I—" Her face turned white as she stared down the hallway. "Merciful heavens," she whispered.

Darcy followed her gaze but noticed nothing save an open door at the end of the hall. However, this signified something to Richard. "That is Edward's room," he said in a strangled voice. His cousin had once told him that his parents kept his brother's room locked up since his death. Darcy had assumed the memories were simply too painful. Was there something else going on?

She rushed along the hallway, and they followed. The richly decorated bedchamber was completely empty. Lady Margaret halted on the threshold, staring in horror at the bed.

"What did you expect to find in Edward's room, Mother?" Richard inquired.

She did not reply; her hand covered her mouth as if to stifle a scream.

Darcy performed a quick circuit of the room with Jane's help, but they found nothing amiss. Richard grabbed his mother's arm and met her gaze. "What was in this room?"

"Edward...Edward was here," she murmured.

"Yes, this was Edward's room." Richard's voice had taken on a patient, cajoling tone. "But Edward is dead. What was here?"

Lady Margaret's eyes focused on her son's face. "Edward *was* here. Your-Your father p-preserved his body here."

Jane emitted a horrified gasp. Richard released his mother's arm, staggering backward. "No! We buried Edward! We buried him at Matlock."

She shook her head. "The c-coffin was empty, w-weighted with sandbags. Your father brought Edward here in secret and preserved him with spells." She gave a faint laugh. "I thought, why not indulge him? He was half-crazed with grief. Having Edward here gave your father peace, prevented him from sinking into despair. We kept it a secret....The servants were ignorant....It hurt nobody."

Richard regarded his mother with wide, horrified eyes. "Mother, the Agency has been seeking a mage—who has killed—a mage who has been practicing necromancy!"

His mother turned even paler. "No. No! Do not say such terrible things! Your father would never—!"

Darcy stood beside his cousin and gestured to the empty room. "This is proof. Uncle Walter *has* been practicing necromancy. He has killed people, raised wights."

She shook her head vigorously. "No. He would not do that."

"No?" Darcy's voice was harsh. "Then where is Edward's body? He would not move it unless he intended to use it. Where is Miss Elizabeth? Uncle Walter must have abducted her."

Tears trickled down his aunt's cheeks. "I do not know where they are. He would not do such things...."

Darcy turned away from her impatiently and faced his cousin. "Do you have any ideas?"

Richard's face was a greenish color. "No...I am caught between castigating myself for not noticing and wishing that I yet remained in ignorance. This is grotesque. What use could he possibly have for Edward's corpse?"

"Can you not guess?" Darcy reigned in his terror to take a gentler tone with his cousin. "He hopes to bring your brother back to life."

Jane nodded slowly. "That is the logical conclusion."

"No...." Lady Margaret moaned and collapsed to the floor. Richard helped her to a chair.

"But why abduct Miss Elizabeth?" Richard asked. "If he wants to prevent her from destroying his wights, he could simply dispose of her." Jane made an anguished noise.

"You told me they were unable to determine how Lady Genevieve perished," Darcy said. "What if he requires a vivomancer to complete the spell?"

"That has a twisted logic to it," Richard said.

"At least we know he will not kill her," Jane said.

"Not yet," Richard said, causing Jane to turn even whiter.

"He needs her for his spell, and I brought her right to his house." Darcy considered banging his head against the wall.

"Time for regrets later," Richard said. "The question is where would he have taken her?"

They all looked at Lady Margaret. Tears streamed down her cheeks. "I do not know. I swear! I thought that all this time he was just visiting his club and mentoring younger mancers." As she continued to sob, Jane helped her from the room and handed her to a maid hovering in the hallway.

Darcy paced the floor, running fingers through already disheveled hair. "They could be anywhere!"

"My father researched necromantic rituals following the wight attack. He might have some thoughts on the subject," Jane volunteered. "Our family arrived at my uncle Gardiner's house this morning. I received the message an hour ago. I could send a note prevailing upon them to join us."

"Please do," Darcy said. "We could make use of their mancy if it comes to a battle." Richard raised his eyebrows, perhaps recalling some of Lydia and Kitty's more egregious conduct. "The Bennets will be an asset in a fight," Darcy assured him. "And Uncle Walter has a small army of followers in addition to the wights."

Jane hurried from the room, calling for a footman to help her send a note.

Richard peered out the window. "No doubt we have a few hours before anything occurs. The necro—my father cannot summon the wights until the sun goes down."

Darcy took a deep breath and reminded himself that Richard was right—despite the inner voice screaming that he must locate Elizabeth immediately.

He nodded to his cousin. "Is there a map of London in the house? We could determine likely places for a necromantic ritual."

"A good thought." Richard strode from the room, and Darcy followed. One way or another they would recover Elizabeth.

* * *

Awareness returned slowly as Elizabeth gradually took in the details of her surroundings. The earl's spell to render her unconscious had been quite effective. She had been laid on a fainting couch in a small office—furnished with a desk, a few chairs, and a fireplace.

As she drifted in and out, Elizabeth recalled and regretted all the decisions that had led her to this moment. Why had she not told Jane when she was investigating the mysterious room at the end of the hallway? Why had she not waited for William before visiting it? For that matter, why had she not suspected Lord Walter before?

And now the earl planned to sacrifice her as part of his twisted scheme to reanimate his son and decimate the Council. She was certain that he schemed to seize power of the Council himself once most of the members were dead. The Council for Enchantment wielded enormous power in Britain. Without any checks on his authority, the earl could do great damage.

Tears leaked from Elizabeth's eyes and rolled down her cheeks. Bad enough that she would die, but her death would serve an evil and destructive purpose. Why had she not allowed William to propose when he longed to? Why had she not insisted upon it? Why had she not confessed her love for him? Many days ago, she had realized she loved him, and yet her pride had constrained her from speaking the words. Now she would never have the opportunity to tell him. For the rest of his life, William would believe that she was ambivalent about him—or worse, still angry about his deception.

The more she considered her circumstances, the angrier she grew at Lord Walter. How dare he take away her chance to tell William she loved him! How dare he remove their chance for happiness!

Anger animated her into a sitting position and sustained her through the ensuing dizziness. Eventually, she was able to leverage herself into an approximation of standing and move about the room, clinging to the furniture for balance.

A glance at the papers on the desk told her this was the earl's own office in the Council building. She ascertained that the door was locked, and the sole window was too small to provide an escape. However, the window did supply a view of the river; unfortunately, Elizabeth was not in a mood to appreciate its beauty. Voices filtered through the office door, but not specific words. Her captors apparently waited in the adjoining sitting room.

Elizabeth might not be able to escape, but surely she might thwart the necromancer's scheme some other way. If only she could warn William! By now, he would have noticed her absence, unless the earl had glibly managed to account for her disappearance. No, William would not fall for such lies.

But how to send a message…?

Elizabeth opened the window as widely as she could and then cast about for nearby birds. Several answered her summons; she chose a plump pigeon, asking it to alight on the windowsill.

At the desk, Elizabeth scribbled a hasty note to William. The most difficult part of the process was showing the pigeon the location of Matlock House and imprinting images of William on its mind. Seeking individual humans went against the nature of birds, and it was something the pigeon did not easily understand. But Elizabeth's magic prevailed.

She had performed this mancy before when sending messages at Longbourn, although she had used it sparingly, finding it distasteful to impose her will on the bird's. But these were dire circumstances.

She curled up the paper, which the pigeon took in its feet. Soon the bird was soaring into the London skies. She hoped it would follow her instructions and not be distracted by an old woman scattering breadcrumbs in the park. *Perhaps I should summon another bird and send a second message, just in case.*

But before Elizabeth could find another bird, the click of the door's lock told her that her captors had come for her. She turned to face her fate.

***

The elegant dining room at Matlock House had become a command center. People spoke in small groups, consulting maps and arcane necromancy texts. Servants wove through the guests, providing tea and biscuits. Lady Margaret had initially objected to the casual use of her fine furniture, but Darcy had simply glared her into submission.

Jane's message to Gracechurch Street had brought not only the entire Bennet family but also Mr. and Mrs. Gardiner, both accomplished mancers. Mr. Gardiner was also a practical, take-charge sort of man—a good counterbalance to Mr. Bennet's indolence.

Bennet had given insights into the conduct of necromancers. One of his books confirmed the theory that Lord Walter could use Elizabeth's powers to raise his son—and further revealed that she would not survive the ritual. William tried not to think about that.

Unfortunately, nobody had any thoughts about where the earl had taken Elizabeth. They knew he would need to draw life energies from many people to fuel the ritual, but London was full of places where crowds would gather.

After more than two hours of no progress, Darcy's nerves were starting to fray. He found himself snapping at Richard and growling at the household staff. When one of the servants opened the front door for a delivery and a pigeon flew into the front hallway, Darcy's patience snapped. As the bird flitted into the dining room, he barely restrained the impulse to curse. "Will someone catch that creature and return it outside!" he shouted.

Two footmen gamely raced around the room attempting to catch a bird that—implausibly—seemed bent on flying straight for Darcy. Chairs were knocked down, and at least one teacup shattered on the floor.

"Wait!" Jane shouted.

The sound of her raised voice was strange enough to draw everyone's undivided attention. She was watching the bird intently. "It holds a paper in its feet! It must be a message from Lizzy."

"She can do that?" Darcy said weakly.

"She has done so before," Jane said absently as she endeavored to coax the bird into her hand. But the creature was intent on Darcy, flying in circles around his head. "She must have sent the message to you," she observed.

Never having befriended a bird before, Darcy regarded the pigeon with some bewilderment. Finally, he held out his cupped hand. The creature immediately alighted on it and dropped the paper.

Once the message was delivered, the bird hopped to the table and helped itself to the remnants of a piece of toast. Lady Margaret opened her mouth to object, but Darcy glowered her into silence. At the moment, he was so in charity with the bird that he would happily have given it an entire roast—if pigeons ate roasts.

He unfurled the message—written in Elizabeth's graceful hand.

William,

I am locked in Matlock's office at the Council building. He intends to kill the Council members during the ritual to open the new season and use their deaths to fuel his son's rebirth. Please make haste.

I may have neglected to tell you that I love you most ardently.

Elizabeth.

Darcy had to blink back tears, knowing she had written the last sentence because she feared she would never have the opportunity to tell him in person. He dropped the paper into his pocket. Nobody else needed to read what Elizabeth had written for his eyes.

"Uncle Walter has taken Miss Elizabeth to the Council chambers. He intends to kill the Council members and use their deaths to bring Edward back to life." The expressions of disgust and horror on the faces around him mirrored Darcy's own sentiments.

Mr. Gardiner glanced out the window. "The sun is beginning to set. We do not have much time."

Darcy strode to the dining room door. "Who will accompany me to the Council building to rescue Miss Elizabeth and stop Lord Walter?"

Everyone surged for the doorway.

"Wait!" Richard cried. "We must have a plan!"

***

They made a strange procession. The sun was just beginning to set as the earl's followers pulled Elizabeth out of his office and tied her hands behind her back with some kind of bespelled cords that prevented her from using her magic. They thrust her into the midst of the mages, some twenty strong, and herded her toward the pier overlooking the Thames, where the Council was beginning the celebration to open a new season.

Elizabeth was unsurprised to discover Wickham by the earl's side. She had expected him to appear, guessing that his persuasive powers had convinced many of the men to follow the necromancer with the fervency of true believers. Wickham surely helped them forget any doubts they might have about Lord Walter's cause.

Elizabeth worried whether her love for William was strong enough to resist Wickham's influence. But the blackguard did not even glance in her direction, apparently deciding her imminent demise meant she was not worth the effort of persuading.

Bringing up the rear of the procession was the litter bearing Edward Fitzwilliam.

Approximately twenty-five Council members were arranged in a semicircle on the pier, where they had been preparing the speeches and ritual words to begin the celebration. They stared at Lord Walter's procession with baffled frustration.

"Matlock, what is this disturbance about?" demanded an ancient and stooped man who Elizabeth guessed was Sir Lloyd, the Council's leader. "If you have a grievance with the Council, you must raise it in a regular meeting."

Elizabeth recognized the Council's second in command, Lady Farha, from illustrations in the paper. Standing in front of the other Council members, she was even blunter with the earl. "This display is hardly in good taste, my lord!"

The necromancer regarded them with a slight smile. "You condemned my son to death—"

"Is that your concern?" a portly man behind Lady Farha blustered. "The matter was debated and voted upon—"

"You condemned my son to death!" Lord Walter's voice rose, drowning out the others. "Now *I* will condemn *you*." He pronounced the words with a decided relish that caused Sir Lloyd to flinch.

"Behold!" The earl threw his arms up in the air.

The last sliver of the sun had disappeared beneath the horizon, and the sky was suddenly full of wights, drowning out all other sounds with the noise of rustling. They descended upon the Council members like a great flock of bats.

Chapter Fifteen

The portly man and a bespectacled fellow beside him were killed almost instantly, too surprised to mount an effective defense. With a shriek, a woman at one end of the semicircle also fell under the onslaught of two wights.

Trained mages, the Council members soon started to fight back with the pyromancy, aquamancy, and other magics at their disposal. They managed to incapacitate many of the creatures, but they were outnumbered. For each wight that the mages managed to bury, sink in the river, or set on fire, another one took its place.

Completely immobilized, Elizabeth could do nothing but watch in sick horror as innocent people fought and died. When the wights managed to kill a mancer and drain their magic, shimmering trails of power fed that energy back to augment the necromancer's magic. Soon he glowed with a yellow radiance as he laughed and exulted in his newfound power.

When the radiance reached its peak, Lord Walter grabbed Elizabeth by her elbow, dragging her to the side of his son's litter. She tried to pull away, but with her arms fastened behind her back, it was impossible.

Trapping her against the litter, the earl placed one hand on Elizabeth's collarbone and took his son's wrist in the other, allowing him to pull power from Elizabeth and infuse it into Edward. Immediately, Elizabeth felt as if her insides were being liquified and extracted through her mouth. She barely muffled a scream of agony at the sensation of being scraped raw. At this rate, she would be drained of her life energy in minutes.

In an attempt to distract herself from the pain, Elizabeth turned her attention to the earl's followers. Some had joined the battle, expressing their dissatisfaction with the Council by helping the wights destroy the mancers. Others were observing the melee, but then many of the bystanders turned their heads toward the city at some sign of movement Elizabeth had not caught.

Peering in that direction, she saw a small group of indistinct figures racing toward the battle. A moment later, she recognized her Uncle Gardiner, Lydia, and Jane at the front of the group. It was an army of Bennets! They were a truly magnificent sight—warriors who would not hesitate to throw themselves into the fray. For the first time, Elizabeth allowed herself to hope.

Within seconds, the ranks of the Council members were reinforced by four Bennet sisters, Elizabeth's father, and Mr. and Mrs. Gardiner, providing new energy to the battle. She did not see William, but surely he was nearby.

Colonel Fitzwilliam approached Lord Walter and stood on the far side of the litter. "Father, this is not the way! I beg you to desist."

"Leave me, Richard!" the earl commanded. "You will be happy enough when your brother is returned to you."

"Edward would not want this," the colonel argued. "And Mother will never speak with you again if you follow through on this plan."

"Begone! Leave me! I have no quarrel with you!" the earl shouted at his son.

From the corner of her eye, Elizabeth saw a flash of silver from a knife that hovered in midair midway between her and the earl. Of course, William was concealed by shadows! With a quick slashing motion, it cut through the cord of energy connecting her to Lord Walter. She fell backward, gasping in relief.

The necromancer whirled around. screaming in inarticulate rage at the loss of power. He destroyed the knife with a blast of light, but he could see nobody to vent his anger upon. Instead, —guessing that his son was part of a distraction—he turned and blasted the colonel with dark power, causing him to stagger backward. However, he remained unharmed. Elizabeth's father must have fashioned a shield for the colonel.

The earl screamed imprecations at his son and leaped over the litter to reach the colonel. His son retreated, drawing the necromancer away— no doubt part of the plan. Elizabeth's attention was distracted when the mancer guard beside her jerked suddenly and mysteriously collapsed as if struck by an invisible assailant.

Then she sensed a gentle tugging at the cords binding her wrists. "'Tis I, my love," breathed a warm voice in her ear. Swathed in shadows, William was freeing her while the colonel drew his father's attention.

The cool steel of a knife blade briefly rested against her wrists before it severed the cords. She shook out her hands to restore the circulation while he drew both of them away from the litter. The shadows cleared, and William stood before her. "My darling," he murmured in her ear. "I cannot apologize enough for my foolishness. I led you right to the necromancer."

She took his hand in hers. "He deceived everyone, William. Do not be uneasy."

"I would prefer to take you to safety, but I do not believe you will allow it."

"You know me too well," she said soberly. "Only a vivomancer can free the wights from the necromancer's control."

He closed his eyes briefly, squeezing her hands. "There are too many! You would be killed before you can reach them all."

He was not wrong. Dozens of the creatures attacked the Council members—several of whom lay still on the grass. The earl had finally neutralized Colonel Fitzwilliam, who had crumpled in a heap near the Council building, and had returned to infusing the stolen life energy into his other son. Edward Fitzwilliam's body had started to glow with an unearthly blue light.

"Lord Walter is the key," she told William. "Stopping him will stop the wights."

He nodded, releasing Elizabeth and turning to his uncle as if he would fight him, but she caught his arm. "I am the only one who can defeat him," she insisted.

"No. Surely—"

"I must attempt it."

"Elizabeth, I cannot lose you!"

From his place by the side of the litter, the earl bellowed to his followers, "Bring me the vivomancer! I must have her to complete the ritual!"

On the other side of the battle, Wickham shouted, "Get the Bennet wench and take her to our leader!"

Several of the necromancer's followers turned and marched toward Elizabeth. She only had seconds to react. "You need to stop Wickham from inciting the followers. That will weaken the earl's power."

William stared grimly at the followers who were approaching. He understood that she could not battle Matlock and his minions simultaneously. "I will stop them and Wickham." A second later, shadows enveloped him. Two seconds later, the approaching mages halted as they were blinded by shadows.

Elizabeth whirled around and raced toward Edward Fitzwilliam's litter. Her lungs labored and her feet stumbled, reminding her that the earl had already drawn copious reserves of energy from her.

She reached the litter, but Lord Walter had cast a shield around the area as he continued to infuse energy into his son's body. Edward was beginning to move his hands and turn his head from side to side. He was indeed coming to life. Elizabeth swallowed bile that threatened to erupt at the sight.

She was out of time, and her own life energies were faltering.

Desperately, she pulled energy from the living things around her—plants, trees, grass—and threw it at the Necromancer's shields. She managed to make a small dent in the shield, but it had little impact otherwise—except for drawing Matlock's attention.

He grinned through the shield's slight distortions. "How good of you to present yourself. I have need of your powers to complete the last step."

"I will give you one last chance to stop. Cease this carnage and repent," she said.

He laughed, throwing his arms wide and gesturing to the mayhem he had set in motion. "Why would I stop now? I will soon achieve everything I have worked for!" Stretching his hand, he grabbed the bodice of Elizabeth's dress and pulled her toward him—through the brief disturbance of his shield. She struggled against his hold, but the wights were augmenting his strength, and she could not dislodge his hand. Within seconds, she was inside the perimeter of his shield, no more capable of escaping than she had been of entering.

"Really, you should surrender, my dear," he sneered. "It will be less painful for you, and the end will be quicker." His magic once again latched onto her vivomancy, draining it like a river of energy pouring from her body. It hurt like he was pulling her lungs out through her ribcage.

Elizabeth struggled to focus her mind despite the pain, searching inside herself for a ball of white light she had created and concealed inside her body. Creating white light with the energy she had pulled from the living things outside the shield was the only way she could conceive of stopping the necromancer.

She had only used white light power once before when she had incapacitated Wickham—who was a far less powerful mancer than the earl. Elizabeth said a silent prayer that this would work. He was, after all, a mage of death, and she wielded the power of life.

Trying to ignore the searing pain, she pushed the light across the small gap between them and encouraged it to infuse itself into the earl's body. His body jerked, his spasming hand released her, and she stumbled to her knees. He staggered backward—his eyes wide with shock as he attempted to understand what was happening. With a swipe of his hands, he cut off the magical stream connecting him to Elizabeth, but it was too late. The bright white life energy was already inside him.

He opened his eyes and fixed his gaze on Elizabeth. "You cannot stop me for long!" he snarled.

Elizabeth had only seconds' warning before the wights descended on her.

***

Leaving Elizabeth to face his uncle had been the most difficult thing Darcy had ever done in his life. But she was correct. Vivomancy was necessary to counteract necromancy—and Darcy needed to fend off Wickham and the minions so Elizabeth could focus on the necromancer.

Before they left Matlock House, Richard had equipped everyone with spells and magical weapons—like the knife Darcy had used to sever Matlock's connection to Elizabeth. He had also acquired useful spells concealed in several rings he now wore. Darcy released a Stunning spell in the faces of the two followers he had blinded with shadows. They slumped to the ground. He hurled a Fireball spell at the next mage he encountered.

Having thwarted Elizabeth's pursuers, Darcy joined the battle between the necromancer's forces and the Council members and their allies. Many of the wights had been buried in dirt, thrown into the Thames, or lit aflame. But he knew from the fight at Longbourn that the creatures were only temporarily immobilized. However, in the meantime, the defenders were mostly struggling against the necromancer's human followers—fighting magic with magic.

Jane swept two of the earl's followers into the river with huge waves while Lydia used a broadsword she had conjured to deflect firebolts thrown by a tall, thin mage. Kitty was dueling another pyromancer, alternating between throwing fireballs and setting fire to the surrounding foliage; both mages were encircled by scorched earth. Mr. Gardiner was using telekinesis to hurl rocks at the offending mancers.

Wickham, the coward, had not joined the fray. He stood on a tree stump as he exhorted the earl's followers to fight and flinched every time the battle came too close to him.

Darcy pulled shadows about himself and crept around the perimeter of the battle, quickly reaching Wickham's boulder. He tore away the concealing shadows as soon as he was standing before the blackguard, startling him into nearly losing his footing.

"Darc—!" The man's scream devolved into a gurgle when Darcy belted him on the chin. He fell backward, hit his head on the rock, went limp, and slithered off the boulder into an awkward heap on the ground.

Darcy wasted no time in tying the man's hands behind his back and then gagging him for good measure—with his own cravat. After Wickham's attack on Elizabeth, Darcy almost wished the blackguard had provided a reason to kill him, but at least his mancy was ended.

The effect on the earl's followers was not instantaneous. But over the course of a few minutes, their will to fight waned. Three men ran away, hoping to lose themselves in London's streets. Two others lost their concentration and were felled by the magical tricks of their opponents. Another two simply surrendered. Added to the number who had already been captured or killed, most of the followers were accounted for.

Darcy had expected the wights to resume their attack on the Council now that they had time to recover from the various magical defenses. But when he searched the skies, he realized the creatures were speeding toward Elizabeth.

The earl's shields had fallen, and Edward had ceased moving. A bright white glow blazed from Elizabeth's hand, pushing inside the earl's chest. He had staggered backward but could not escape from it.

However, she could not defend herself from the wights and sustain her attack on the earl. Seeing the intense concentration on her face, Darcy very much feared that she would not even notice the wights until it was too late. "To Elizabeth!" he shouted to the others as he raced toward her. "Protect Elizabeth! She fights the necromancer!"

He cast shadows even as he ran, blinding the first wight to reach Elizabeth. The second scored a long bloody scratch down her arm, causing her to flinch, but she did not look away from the earl. Fortunately, Kitty was there to ignite the creature. Richard had staggered to Elizabeth's side and managed to stab the next one with his sword.

The earl screamed for help from his followers, not realizing that they had deserted him.

Then Bennet, his face red with exertion, reached Elizabeth and cast a quick shield spell over her, repelling even the most determined wights. Darcy grinned. Their fierce defense of Elizabeth allowed her to focus her attention on the earl.

The white light had incapacitated Matlock, but he was still in command of his magic and still controlling the wights, a truly unstoppable force. Then Darcy noticed the amulet around Lord Walter's neck—the same amulet Darcy had stolen weeks ago. It gleamed with a baleful red glow. Darcy knew the necromancer needed it to create wights, but why would it glow now—in the midst of battle?

That is how he binds the wights! He had needed the amulet to summon the creatures, and he used it to keep them trapped in the physical world.

"Elizabeth!" he cried. "Destroy the amulet!"

Without hesitation, she pointed to the amulet and pulsed life energy into it. Matlock tried to turn away, but he was too late. The white light caught inside the amulet's red stone, creating a fiery blaze so bright that Darcy was forced to avert his eyes.

As a tool of necromancy, the amulet was certainly not designed to contain such vivomancy. The earl yanked at the chain holding the amulet as if it burned him, but before he could rid himself of it, the amulet burst into an eerie red fire—as though flames devoured the medallion from the inside.

Waves of magical power spread out from the amulet like ripples in a pond. As the ripples washed over the wights, they desisted their attacks, losing focus and flying aimlessly around the sky.

The red flames themselves soon crept out of the amulet, spreading to consume the fabric of the earl's tunic, producing agonizing screams. The fire burrowed into the flesh underneath—behaving as no natural fire would. Lord Walter shrieked as mystical flames spread down his legs and along his arms. Within seconds, his body began to crumble into ashes until even his head and face had disappeared. Soon nothing remained of the necromancer's body but a pile of dust.

Only then did Darcy think to glance around—and noted that all of the wights had disappeared. The trapped souls were now free. On the litter, Edward's flesh crumbled away, leaving behind bare, desiccated bones.

Elizabeth's face was blackened by soot and dirt; wisps of hair escaped her coiffure, and her dress was rumpled and torn. But Darcy had never seen anyone more beautiful. He closed the few feet between them and enfolded her in his arms. She leaned against him, trembling with exhaustion and nerves. "I k-killed him…" she murmured into Darcy's chest.

He smoothed the curls that had escaped her pins. "You destroyed the amulet. You could not have foreseen it would kill him."

"Still, I was the instrument of his death."

"You had no choice, my love. And you saved many lives."

She rested more of her weight against him until he was practically holding her in a standing position. "At least the souls of those wights are now free," she said.

"Yes. That is a blessing."

They were silent for a long moment. Elizabeth closed her eyes and breathed deeply, enjoying the moment of peace.

"My love?" Darcy murmured.

"Yes?"

"Your father and uncle are approaching, and I believe they do not approve of the familiar way in which I am holding you."

Muffled giggles vibrated against his chest.

"Will you do me the honor of being my wife?"

Pulling a little away from him, Elizabeth met his gaze. "Do you suppose these are the ideal circumstances for an offer of marriage, William?" she inquired archly.

He shrugged with a smile. "I fear our lives have conspired to prevent ideal circumstances."

She heaved a pretend sigh. "Very well. I will marry you. But someday I would like a lovely marriage proposal."

He chuckled. "Perhaps on our honeymoon." He bent his head to kiss her.

Epilogue

Bells chimed incessantly as Darcy led Elizabeth, her hand tucked into the crook of his arm, down the aisle to the church door. Wedding guests clapped and cheered. The church was full to overflowing with family, friends, and a fair number of people Darcy did not recognize.

This was not how he had imagined his wedding. He had envisioned a small ceremony at the Kympton church or perhaps wherever his bride's family resided. He had not expected a big society wedding in the heart of London, but events had overtaken him and Elizabeth.

Footmen opened the church doors to reveal still more crowds of people waiting outside. Townspeople jostled for positions where they could secure a glimpse of the newly married couple. The noise was deafening as people cheered and vendors hawked food.

He and Elizabeth still found their fame rather fantastical.

One of the surviving Council members was the owner of a prominent London paper who found the story of the "Battle of Westminster" extremely newsworthy. News of the event spread like wildfire throughout London and ultimately the whole country. Elizabeth and her family were credited with saving London, nay all of Britain, from the depredations of an evil necromancer hiding among the aristocracy.

Sensationalist—and often inaccurate—descriptions of the battle had been featured in newspapers for weeks—with accompanying illustrations of Elizabeth and the others fighting hordes of wights. The Council, embarrassed that one of their members had turned out to be a necromancer, had encouraged the celebration of Elizabeth's prowess to demonstrate that all mancers were not evil and that some could be beneficial to the country. Elizabeth and Darcy themselves had remained rather secluded and done nothing to encourage this adulation, but it had fed on itself.

Elizabeth had been inundated with invitations to balls and soirees. Everyone in the *ton* longed to claim her acquaintance. Although Aunt Margaret was still in mourning for her husband, she was eagerly taking credit for having "discovered" the diamond of the first water who was Elizabeth Bennet. What a wonderful revenge on Uncle Walter; Darcy almost wished the man was alive to witness it.

When the papers had learned that Elizabeth had accepted Darcy's proposal of marriage, their love story had become intertwined with the story of their heroism, becoming even more irresistible. Ironically, just as

Darcy had ceased to care about society's opinion over his choice of wife, they were tripping over each other to sing her praises. More than one man about town had told Darcy how clever he was to have secured her affection. He could only laugh.

The Bennet family was now lauded in Hertfordshire, and Bingley was considered quite prescient for proposing to Jane immediately after the events in London. Kitty and Lydia—and even Mary—were plied with invitations to balls and dinners. Mr. Collins related to Lady Catherine's dinner guests that he once had the privilege of singing a marriage proposal to the great Elizabeth Bennet.

Elizabeth's popularity had even exerted pressure upon St. James's Palace to recognize her heroism. The Prince Regent had paused his partying long enough to invite Darcy and Elizabeth to hold their wedding banquet at the palace. They could not refuse.

Now three royal carriages awaited the wedding party outside the door to the church. They would carry the new Mr. and Mrs. Darcy, along with their assorted family members, to the palace for what promised to be a far greater wedding breakfast than they had ever envisioned. Townspeople lined up to follow the procession—transforming it into an impromptu parade. Darcy could only hope they would not provide too much disruption to London's traffic.

He helped Elizabeth into the first carriage. Mr. and Mrs. Bennet and the Gardiners would occupy the second carriage while the third would hold Georgiana and Elizabeth's sisters. Richard would ride alongside on a magnificent stallion.

While Darcy was exceedingly grateful that Elizabeth had secured the recognition and acceptance she so richly deserved, the whole wedding process had been exhausting. He could not wait until tomorrow—when they would enjoy some privacy.

Elizabeth waved to the crowds as the carriage sprang forward. Darcy indicated the small bouquet of flowers in her lap. "Do you like the blooms I chose for you?"

"Indeed. They are lovely," she said. "But I do not understand why you insisted on being the one to provide my bouquet."

He gave her an arch smile. "You opined that flowers were an acceptable means for expressing my gratitude for saving my life."

Elizabeth laughed. "Marriage is a rather roundabout way of supplying me with flowers!"

"Hmm. Your father said something similar. He inquired if our marriage is a roundabout way of repaying your family for their care and hospitality."

"Surely he was joking," Elizabeth said.

Darcy shrugged. "I am never certain with your father. I simply assured him of my deep and ardent love for you."

"Do you still believe we should have eloped?" she asked him with a smile. When the public attention toward their wedding had grown nearly unbearable, Darcy had suggested a quick visit to Scotland.

He chuckled at their shared joke. "It would have been the perfect solution. You are so eager to travel."

"You would not have been able to present me with such a bouquet," she said, indicating her lovely hothouse flowers.

"Ah! I had a plan for an even more unique collection of flowers," he said.

She leaned toward him. "I am intrigued...."

Darcy held out his hand and concentrated. The trick had taken a great deal of practice to get just right. Soon a bouquet of perfectly formed shadow flowers appeared.

Elizabeth's lips parted. "Oh my!" She reached out and then withdrew her hand as she realized the bouquet had no substance. "It is beautiful! Thank you."

"These flowers will never wither and die—and we may take them with us wherever we go."

Her eyes were still fixed on the shadow blossoms. "Let us bring them on the honeymoon!"

"Certainly. I will happily provide them whenever you would like." Waving away the bouquet, he took her hand and kissed it. They had planned a honeymoon of several months that would take them to Ireland, Scotland, and many parts of England that Elizabeth had never seen. Darcy was almost as excited about it as she was.

She rested her head against his shoulder. "I cannot wait for it to begin."

Darcy was hardly less eager. "It will be quite a welcome respite before our duties descend upon us," he observed. They had both been offered positions on the Council—which had been sadly decimated by Matlock. Darcy had accepted with alacrity, but Elizabeth had agreed only on the condition that the Council institute new policies to protect vivomancers.

She suspected there were other vivomancers hidden in Britain who refused to identify themselves for the same reasons she had. Upon their return, she intended to start a Council-sponsored program to identify, train, and protect vivomancers so they could become a valuable resource for the country while ensuring their safety. The crown's approval of Elizabeth made it difficult for the Council to refuse her proposal.

"There is another project I am eager to start as well," Elizabeth said, giving him a mischievous smile.

"What is that?" Darcy asked warily. They would be quite busy running Pemberley and performing Council duties. He was not eager to take on additional responsibilities.

She snuggled next to him. "Well, you know, vivomancers excel at nurturing living beings...."

"Yes." Darcy frowned. "Would you like to get a puppy?"

Elizabeth laughed. "No. I thought we might see how a vivomancer is at *creating* new life."

It took Darcy a moment to catch her meaning. "I heartily support that plan."

The End

Thank you for purchasing this book. I know you have many entertainment options, and I appreciate your spending your time with my story. Support from readers like you makes it possible for independent authors like me to continue writing.

Reviews are a book's lifeblood.

Please consider leaving a review where you purchased the book.

Learn more about me and my upcoming releases:

Sign up for my newsletter: *Dispatches from Pemberley*

Website: www.victoriakincaid.com

Blog: https://kincaidvictoria.wordpress.com/

Facebook: https://www.facebook.com/kincaidvictoria

Please enjoy this excerpt from Chapter one of **Mages and Mysteries**, another Pride and Prejudice Fantasy Variation by Victoria Kincaid

In Regency England, women are expected to confine their magical acts to mending dresses or enhancing their beauty, but Elizabeth Bennet insists on crafting her own spells to fight goblins and protect the people of Meryton. She even caused a scandal by applying for admission to the magical Academy. When Hertfordshire is beset with a series of unexplained goblin attacks, Elizabeth is quite ready to protect her family and friends. If only she didn't have to deal with the attitude of the arrogant mage, Fitzwilliam Darcy.

Mr. Darcy doesn't need to be associated with a scandalous woman like Elizabeth Bennet—no matter how attractive she is. But as the goblin attacks accelerate and grow more dangerous, Darcy realizes that he could use her help in identifying the cause—and is forced to recognize her magical ability. Unfortunately, continued proximity to Elizabeth only heightens his attraction to her—which is particularly inconvenient in light of his engagement to Caroline Bingley.

Can Elizabeth and Darcy unravel the mystery of the goblin attacks before more people are hurt? And how can they manage their growing mutual attraction? It's sure to be interesting...because when Darcy and Elizabeth come together, magic happens.

Chapter One

The dancing nymphs were not equal to Caroline Bingley's standards. "Hmph," she sniffed. "Their dancing could be more graceful. And their dresses do not even glow."

Bingley gave her a carefully correct smile—the smile he used when he tried not to contradict his sister. "I suppose there are fewer nymph dancing troupes to hire in Hertfordshire than in town."

Caroline gave an elegant shrug. "Then they should do without. It is not as if nymph dancers are *de rigeur* at an assembly ball in the country."

"I suppose the good people of Hertfordshire are showing everyone how sophisticated they are. Nymph dancing troupes must surely be a novelty here." Louisa Hurst tittered with her sister.

"Or perhaps they take pleasure in watching the nymphs dance. They are quite lovely," Bingley said with absolute sincerity.

Darcy silently agreed with his friend. Small and light, nymphs could perform tricks and elegant dance steps that would be impossible for a human. The troupe at the Meryton assembly was perhaps not the most sophisticated he had ever observed, but they wove intricate and beautiful patterns with ribbons. Darcy said nothing to Caroline; he was less willing than Bingley to draw her wrath.

The party from Netherfield watched in silence as the performance concluded with an elaborate pose made colorful by ribbons wrapped around each dancer's wrists. Darcy joined the applause; the dancers should be commended just for avoiding tangling up the ribbons.

The five nymph dancers glided to the edge of the dais that occupied one end of the assembly hall and made elegant bows before hurrying out the door. Although they took delight in performing for humans, nymphs tended to be shy and uninterested in socializing with other species. The members of a small orchestra—all human—swept onto the dais and commenced tuning their instruments.

Caroline was not finished punishing her brother for the sin of prevailing upon them to attend a country dance. "Have you noticed the pathetic attempt at décor?" She waved negligently at the ceiling. "Colored flames in the chandeliers? Shadow silhouettes on the walls? It is all so passe. The floral decorations do not sparkle. And the curtains have been blue all evening. The least they could do is enchant the curtains!" Her eyes slid toward Darcy. "Surely you agree with me."

He hated to be drawn into a disagreement between the siblings, but honesty—and a sense of obligation to Caroline— compelled him to respond. "The décor does rather possess an amateur air," he admitted. Colored flames and enchanted silhouettes on the walls had been popular in London three years ago, but the most fashionable balls now had more sophisticated decor.

Bingley was not perturbed by the criticism. "I find it most charming. The decorations were probably conjured by a local mage in his spare time. They would not possess the funds to hire a professional decorator mage."

"That much is exceedingly obvious," Caroline sneered.

Bingley's attention was drawn toward movement on the far side of the room. Sir William Lucas, one of the local landowners, was moving toward them purposefully with other local residents in his wake.

"Apparently Sir William has other people for us to meet," Bingley said with relish. Darcy managed not to groan; meeting people had to be the most tedious part of attending balls.

"I thank you for my share of the favor," Caroline drawled, "but I am forced to decline. I have an urgent need to visit the ladies' retiring room." Grabbing her sister's arm, Caroline fled the scene as if being chased by enemy soldiers. Hurst, Louisa's husband, had already taken himself off to the card room, leaving Darcy standing with Bingley and cursing himself for not having affected an escape earlier.

Just as Sir William reached them, the orchestra struck up a lively dance tune. "Mr. Bingley! Mr. Darcy!" The man's voice was always quite a bit louder than the occasion warranted. He gestured expansively toward the family of worthies arrayed behind him. "Allow me to introduce the Bennet family. Mr. and Mrs. Bennet and three of their daughters, Miss Jane Bennet, Miss Elizabeth Bennet, and Miss Mary Bennet. Their younger two daughters have already found dancing partners."

Everyone exchanged bows and curtsies. Bingley's gaze lingered on Miss Jane Bennet, who was quite lovely, with a blonde halo of hair framing a serenely beautiful countenance. Darcy's attention was particularly arrested by Elizabeth Bennet. Her hair was a mass of dark curls, and her smile held a faint hint of amusement in it. *How intriguing.* Something about her name was familiar, but Darcy would remember meeting a woman of such striking beauty.

Mrs. Bennet burbled about how wonderful it was to see such fine young men at their "fair assembly." By "fine," Darcy understood her to mean "wealthy." He was accustomed to this reaction, but that did not render it less tedious.

While the others spoke of inconsequential subjects, the question of where Darcy had heard of Elizabeth Bennet nagged at him. When Mr. Bennet said something about the Academy of Magic, Darcy remembered. "Miss Elizabeth, are you the woman who petitioned the Convocation for admission to the Academy?" He blurted out the words.

She did not appear nearly as abashed as he would have expected. "I am, but that was three years ago. I am intrigued to find that you still recognize my name."

"I was part of the Convocation panel that heard your petition." Only after uttering those words did Darcy realize it was hardly the most politic thing he could have said. The panel had been unanimous in rejecting her application; the Academy had never admitted a woman.

Fortunately, she appeared more amused than irritated. "It is a shame the panel did not see fit to test my magical abilities before denying my request. That might have altered their opinion." Darcy expected the other mages in the group to be embarrassed by this forwardness, but her father laughed an agreement and Sir William nodded. The sisters regarded Miss Elizabeth with sympathy. Only Mrs. Bennet colored and glanced away. Apparently Miss Elizabeth's application to study magic was well known in the community. *How curious.*

"Magical studies in the Academy are quite rigorous and even dangerous," Darcy said. "They should not be undertaken lightly."

"I assure you, I had every intention of undertaking them quite heavily." Her father snorted a laugh and even Bingley smiled.

Darcy's friend broke the ensuing awkward silence by inviting Miss Bennet to dance the next set, which was just beginning to form. After her shy agreement, they hurried toward the dance floor. Politeness suggested that Darcy prevail upon Miss Elizabeth to dance, but he could not bring himself to do so. She had created a minor scandal, and he had no intention of associating himself with her any longer than the length of the discussion. Obviously she rated herself rather highly if she believed her abilities equal to the most talented young mages in the country.

"I understand you are from Derbyshire, sir?" Mrs. Bennet asked.

"Yes, my estate is Pemberley—near Matlock," Darcy answered shortly. Questions about his income hovered unspoken in the air. Darcy wondered if there were a polite way to hint at how fruitless any matrimonial efforts would be. Mrs. Bennet babbled about a distant relative from Lambton, relieving Darcy of any social obligations save nodding at appropriate moments.

Everyone knew that women's magic was better suited to small domestic tasks such as mending clothing, embroidery, or beautifying charms. Female servants might use a little magic to enhance food they made, make cleaning easier, or light a kitchen fire. However, most women were not adept with higher level spells.

History did offer a few exceptions to this rule, such as the notorious Jane Dee during Elizabeth I's reign. But customarily women did not possess the capacity for greater magic, leaving male mages to fight magical wars and perform other dangerous tasks.

Darcy understood why Miss Elizabeth was without a dance partner despite her beauty. If the woman's doomed application was widely known in the neighborhood, scandal would have attached to the whole family.

Citing the need for some punch, Darcy turned and hastened away from the group. This assembly ball was tedious enough; he did not need to struggle through an awkward discourse with such a family.

Caroline Bingley was standing near the punch table, and Darcy hastened to pour her a glass. She accepted with a smile. "Thank you, Fitzwilliam, you are so thoughtful."

"The prospects for good society are not promising," he replied. "We must rely upon each other for company."

"Indeed." She laughed as if he had said something exceedingly droll. "Only our *own* company is tolerable." She regarded him with an expectant expression.

Oh. "Would you honor me with the next dance?" Darcy asked.

"I would be delighted," she drawled.

Darcy occasionally had small reservations about Caroline's character; she could be cutting and cold. But she had excellent taste in fashion, and nobody could fault her manners. In addition, the Bingleys were a well-established magical family with Convocation members stretching back for generations—although Bingley's father had unfortunately dabbled in trade to replenish the family's coffers.

Nevertheless, Darcy had made the right decision when he had prevailed upon Caroline to marry him.

After two sets with his fiancée, Darcy had retreated from the dance floor. Caroline had taken herself off to the ladies' retiring room once again, and Mrs. Hurst was dancing with a militia officer.

If only he could depart without causing a minor scandal! Their party had been in Hertfordshire less than a week, and they were not acquainted with many people in the room. Balls were such a colossal waste of time. Netherfield was not the most stimulating place, but there Darcy could read the latest magical journals or write a letter to his sister Georgiana. In fact, he would have preferred not to visit Hertfordshire at all, but he had been powerless to deny entreaties from both Bingley and Caroline.

Darcy was considering yet another glass of punch when Bingley appeared at his side. His friend was always in his element amidst a large crowd of people—perpetually well liked wherever he went. Darcy occasionally envied his friend's easy ways but found them onerous at other times. This event fell into the latter category.

"Come Darcy, I hate to see you standing about by yourself in this stupid manner," Bingley declared. "I must have you dance."

"I certainly shall not," Darcy said. "You know how I detest it unless I am particularly acquainted with my partner. Your sisters are engaged, and there is not another woman in the room whom it would not be a punishment to stand up with."

"I have never met so many pleasant girls and several of them are uncommonly pretty," Bingley said.

Darcy had already been importuned into visiting Hertfordshire and attending this vexing dance. He was not about to allow himself to be coerced into additional dancing. "You are dancing with the only handsome girl in the room," Darcy said, indicating Miss Bennet.

"Oh! She is the most beautiful creature I ever beheld! But, there is one of her sisters who is very pretty and, I dare say, very agreeable." Bingley waved his hand toward their right.

Darcy turned his head just enough; Miss Elizabeth stood not far away. He had to admit that she was quite lovely—with particularly fine dark eyes. She regarded him with an enigmatic smile.

He quickly glanced away. Apparently the Darcy fortune would easily overcome any reservations the woman had about his role on the Convocation panel. But Darcy's reservations were not so easily conquered. Even if he were not engaged, he would not be inclined to give her any encouragement.

"She is tolerable," Darcy said to Bingley, "but not handsome enough to tempt me." She could not fail to overhear, which was all to the good; she was less likely to importune him. "I am in no humor at present to give consequence to women with such insufferably high self-regard."

Bingley laughed uncomfortably. "I would not be as fastidious as you for a kingdom! I understand why the panel denied her application, but surely there is no harm in *desiring* to attend the Academy."

"You know what the Academy is like," Darcy said. "She would not have lasted a single day. There was no reason for the Convocation to indulge her capricious ambitions."

Bingley shrugged. "Perhaps not, but there is also no reason to avoid dancing with her." His friend gave Darcy no opportunity to reply. "Perhaps Miss Jane Bennet might agree to another dance."

A moment after Bingley's departure, Darcy happened to glance to his right; Miss Elizabeth Bennet had quitted the vicinity. It was just as well. Her presence had been annoying, and those eyes had been a distraction.

***

Jane will be pleased to hear that Mr. Bingley thinks she is the most beautiful creature he ever beheld. Since Elizabeth had no hopes of a partner for the dance, she might as well relate something that would lift her sister's spirits. Since men were scarce at the assembly, Elizabeth had briefly harbored hopes that one of the newcomers to Hertfordshire might dance with her, but Mr. Darcy had dashed that dream quite thoroughly.

She took pleasure in dancing and had no additional expectations for any partner. But since her aspirations for Academy admission had become widely known, many of the young men in Hertfordshire had taken to avoiding her. Certainly "tolerable" was not the worst insult she had ever heard.

A sigh escaped Elizabeth. She did not regret applying to the Academy; she was more than qualified. But occasionally she regretted that her reputation deprived her of an opportunity to dance.

As she crossed the room, she felt a tug on her magical senses that warned her someone was manipulating the ether in the room. It did not take much searching for her to find Lydia on one side of the room coaxing strands of ether to create a small gust of wind that blew one of the militia officer's hats across the floor. Every time the poor officer drew near the hat, it blew away again—while Kitty and the other militia officers laughed. Apparently the poor man did not command enough magic to counter Lydia's; no wonder he had joined the militia.

Lydia was the most magically talented of Elizabeth's sisters, but she never used it to any purpose—regarding it as merely another tool in her perpetual quest for "some laughs." None of their father's chastisements curtailed Lydia's misuse of magic.

At least Elizabeth could benefit the hapless officer. With a flick of her wrist, she yanked on the strands of ether that Lydia manipulated, causing the wind to reverse itself so the hat landed on the startled militia officer's head. Lydia immediately spied who had thwarted her amusement. "Lizzy!" She stamped her foot and scowled at her older sister.

Lydia never considered the consequences of her actions. Elizabeth drew her sister away from the others. "You were creating a spectacle," she said in a low tone.

Her sister rolled her eyes. "We were only having a laugh! Even Denny was laughing!"

Elizabeth folded her arms over her chest. "Are you bent on achieving a reputation as a girl who misuses magic?"

"I don't care!" Lydia pouted.

"Be that as it may. If you do not cease at once I will follow you around the ballroom and negate every one of your silly spells."

Lydia's chin jutted upward belligerently, but she knew Elizabeth was not making an empty threat. "I would hate to deprive you of the opportunity to dance," she said in a falsely sweet voice. "Oh, wait, *nobody* will dance with you."

Elizabeth forced herself not to react. "Keep this up and nobody will dance with *you*." She gave her sister a quelling glance.

Lydia tossed her head and turned on her heel. Returning to her group of friends, she grabbed the hand of the officer closest to her. "Come, let's go dance!" The man grinned, apparently undeterred by her forwardness, and accompanied her to the dance floor.

Elizabeth found Jane near the punch table. Her countenance was serenely beautiful as always, but her eyes sparkled with an unusual brightness. "Did you enjoy dancing with Mr. Bingley?" Elizabeth inquired.

"He is quite gracious, a true gentleman." Despite her measured words, Jane was obviously fighting to hide a smile.

Elizabeth took her sister's hand and squeezed it; rarely had she seen her sister so ebullient. "I *may* have overheard Mr. Bingley relate that you are the most beautiful creature he had ever beheld."

Her sister gave a very un-Jane-like giggle and immediately clapped a hand over her mouth. "It is wrong to eavesdrop, Lizzy," she said with mock sincerity.

"It is not eavesdropping if they are speaking loudly enough."

Jane peered closely at her sister. "I saw his friend watching you. I thought he might prevail upon you to dance."

"Watching *me*? You must have been mistaken. Mr. Darcy is not as gallant as Mr. Bingley, I fear. He declined an opportunity to dance with me because—" She imitated the man's deep tones. "I am in no mood to give consequence to women with such insufferably high self-regard."

"He said that?" Jane was more horrified than Elizabeth had been. "To say such a thing in your hearing is very wrong."

Elizabeth shrugged. Jane had no notion of how frequently people said far worse. "You know I am not seeking a husband." She was not averse to marriage, but she had resigned herself to the possibility of dying a spinster. Most days it did not bother her, although she was occasionally apprehensive that she would feel differently in ten years.

"In any case," Elizabeth said briskly. "I am far more unhappy that Mr. Darcy denied my admission to the Academy than I am over any slight at a ball." The injustice of the Convocation's refusal still rankled. The panel had not even been willing to test her to determine if she had sufficient magical talent. Elizabeth did not have unjustifiably high regard for her own abilities, but she had met many Academy graduates with far less skill than she possessed.

Jane nodded. "It was wrong for them to deny you."

"I daresay I will not languish for the want of Mr. Darcy's friendship," Elizabeth said with a laugh. "He is clearly a man to make quick judgments."

"Perhaps he spoke in haste and is now regretting it," Jane said. "Perhaps he will invite you to dance later."

"I think I can promise you that I will never dance with Mr. Darcy."

A commotion at the ballroom's entrance drew their attention. "Goblin! There is a goblin on the drive!" A coachman shouted as he raced into the room.

The music stuttered to a halt. Elizabeth regarded the coachman skeptically. Goblin appearances were rare—and usually a result of storms. The sky today could not be clearer. Perhaps the coachman had mistaken a bear or wolf for a goblin. "What sort of goblin?" someone shouted at the man.

He shrugged. "Big—at least six feet tall—and blue!"

People gasped all over the ballroom. *Very well. Definitely not a wolf or bear.*

Another servant entered at a run shouting the same thing, prompting an older lady to faint, a singularly unhelpful reaction to the news. Some guests surged toward the doors—running for the terrace or escaping elsewhere in the building—as others shouted that the ballroom doors should be barricaded.

Two figures emerged from the back of the ballroom and swept past Elizabeth: Mr. Bingley and Mr. Darcy. The latter was unsheathing a sword engraved with runes: a bespelled blade.

Jane's hand flew to her mouth. "Oh! They must be paladins." The warrior mages were the kingdom's primary defense against goblin attacks, evil mages, and any other dark magic that might threaten the rest of the population. Paladins learned a special technique that allowed them to hide and then summon their swords seemingly from thin air.

Elizabeth rolled her eyes. *"Of course* Mr. Darcy is a paladin." They were known for an extra helping of arrogance.

Jane watched Mr. Bingley disappear through the ballroom door. "We are fortunate they are here."

Elizabeth had never observed a paladin fight; goblins and other dark magic were rare in Hertfordshire. Watching the battle would be terribly thrilling. But fighting goblins was hardly an activity that called for spectators, and her assistance might be needed in the ballroom.

"Remain calm!" shouted a stout, unprepossessing man who emerged from the card room. Since Elizabeth did not recognize him, she guessed he was another visitor from Netherfield. "If you remain within the ballroom, you will be safe. I am a mage with the Convocation, and I shall fight any goblins that attempt to attack this room!"

There was a general murmur of approbation at this announcement, but Elizabeth was tempted to roll her eyes. *Most* mages belonged to the Convocation—well, male mages anyway—the country's magical governing body. Being a member did not prove much beyond a minimal level of magical talent.

The man chanted in Latin to activate a spell. Elizabeth could sense him weaving together strands of ether—the magical energy that only mages could see or use. He created a standard deflection spell, which would be useful if anyone shot arrows into the room but would do little to stop a goblin.

When the man ceased chanting, several people applauded, causing the stout man to preen. Elizabeth sighed. Yet another Academy-trained mage who regarded himself more highly than was warranted.

Somebody yanked on Elizabeth's arm, and she turned. Her hands fluttering like butterflies, Elizabeth's mother peered anxiously at her. "Your father went to summon the carriage. The goblin will attack him, I know it! What shall we do if he is killed? We'll be thrown into the hedgerows for sure."

"Papa is outside?" A stab of terror jolted through Elizabeth.

She took a step toward the door, but Jane caught her hand. "You cannot go outside, Lizzy. It is too dangerous!"

"It is not much safer here," Elizabeth replied. "That mage could not stop an angry gnome."

"Let the paladins take care of it," Jane insisted, her forehead creased with worry.

"I will not leave Papa alone and defenseless," Elizabeth said. The mere mention of her father provoked an anguished moan from her mother. "The paladins may not even know he is there." Without another word, she pulled her arm from Jane's grasp and rushed toward the door.

Guests were wailing in fear or arguing loudly about what to do; the commotion made it easy for Elizabeth to slip through the doorway unnoticed. The last thing she needed was someone trying to prevent her from leaving for her own good.

The corridors were empty; no doubt the servants were hiding. The sounds of shouting and the goblin's angry roar echoed through the building even before Elizabeth reached the front hall. Despite her slippers and long gown, Elizabeth crossed the hall quickly and burst through the doors to a little porch, which topped a short flight of stone stairs that descended to the drive. She stopped to take stock of a scene that barely made sense.

It was a warm night for early January, but winter's bite was still in the air. The sun had set long ago, but a plethora of torches illuminated the circular drive before the assembly hall. The drive was lined with coaches; the coachmen had fled. The goblin stood on the roof of a ruined carriage, having killed the horses with swipes from its enormous claws.

Elizabeth was astonished at how accurate the terrified coachman's description had been. The monster was at least six feet tall—with bright blue, leathery skin covered in thick dark hair and twisted horns emerging from its skull. Most notably, it had six arms that each ended in five-inch claws. Elizabeth had only encountered one goblin previously, and it had resembled a cross between a hellhound and a border collie—with a tendency to eat sheep rather than herd them. This goblin was nothing like that.

But she had viewed similar illustrations in books. "Hobgoblin," she breathed. Her stomach lurched with agitation—and a touch of excitement. Many mages went their whole lives without observing a hobgoblin, one of the most destructive types of goblins.

Given its size, she was not surprised that Mr. Bingley and Mr. Darcy were struggling to fight it. Just after she emerged from the hall, the goblin jumped down from the roof of the ruined coach, forcing Mr. Bingley to jump backward to avoid being sliced open by one long claw.

Mr. Darcy fared a little better. Needing to stay out of reach of the six long arms, he struggled to get close enough to the creature to stab it. While the goblin's attention was distracted by Mr. Bingley, Mr. Darcy did manage to land one good blow, severing one of its hands. The goblin screamed in pain, but did not slow its attack, advancing with even more fury. The stump at the end of its arm bled freely for a few seconds, but then a hand started to grow back. Heavens! How unfair! How could such a creature be defeated?

Elizabeth had a tendency to dive headlong into any fray but held herself back from racing toward the goblin by sheer power of will. She reminded herself that paladins were trained for such battles, and she was not. Moreover, her task was to find her father. She strained her eyes but could discern no figure lurking in the shadows along the edge of the drive. Her breath caught in her throat. *Where was he? Had the goblin already killed him?*

Then she spied a figure, crumpled and unmoving, at the foot of the steps.

About Victoria Kincaid

The author of more than sixteen best-selling Regency and modern *Pride and Prejudice* variations, Victoria Kincaid has a Ph.D. in English literature and runs a small business, er, household with two children, a hyperactive dog, an overly affectionate cat, and a husband who is not threatened by Mr. Darcy. They live near Washington DC, where the inhabitants occasionally stop talking about politics long enough to complain about the traffic.

On weekdays Victoria is a writer who specializes in IT marketing (it's more interesting than it sounds). In her past as a freelance writer, some of her more…unusual writing subjects have included space toilets, laser gynecology, orthopedic shoes, generating energy from onions, Ferrari rental car services, and vampire face lifts (she swears she is not making any of this up). She is also the host of the annual Jane Austen Fan Fiction Reader/Writer Get Together and confesses to an extreme partiality for the 1995 version of *Pride and Prejudice.*

Books by Victoria Kincaid:

Darcy and Deception

Darcy's Honor

The Secrets of Darcy and Elizabeth

Pride and Proposals

Mr. Darcy to the Rescue

Darcy vs. Bennet

Chaos Comes to Longbourn

Christmas at Darcy House

A Very Darcy Christmas

When Jane Got Angry

When Mary Met the Colonel

When Charlotte Became Romantic

The Unforgettable Mr. Darcy

President Darcy

Darcy Goes to Hollywood

Rebellion at Longbourn